"You've just sold me on it completely!"

Olivia laughed as she said this.

"No quibble about wages?" Ross questioned.

"The man saves me from my creditors, gives me a job and a roof over my head, and now he wants to *pay* me?" Olivia asked a fat china Buddha sitting on top of a nearby bookcase.

"The laborer is worthy, etcetera," Ross reminded her piously.

"Great, but you've got to accept a little gratitude. You've been an absolute savior. And Ross—will you explain *why* you're doing all this for me?"

He sighed and looked at her, his dark blue eyes flickering with hidden mirth.

"It would be so much easier to seduce you if we were living together," he said simply, and waited for her reaction....

Dear Reader:

We hope our December Harlequin Romances bring you many hours of enjoyment this holiday season.

1989 was an exciting year. We published our 3000th Harlequin Romance! And we introduced a new cover design—which we hope you like.

We're wrapping up the year with a terrific selection of satisfying stories, written by your favorite authors, as well as by some very talented newcomers we're introducing to the series. As always, we've got settings guaranteed to take you places—from the English Cotswolds, to New Zealand, to Holland, to some hometown settings in the United States.

So when you need a break from the hustle and bustle of preparing for the holidays, sit back and relax with our heartwarming stories. Stories with laughter...a few tears...and lots of heart.

And later, when you get a chance, drop us a line with your thoughts and ideas about how we can try to make your enjoyment of Harlequin Romances even better in the years to come.

From our house to yours, Happy Holidays! And may this special season bring you a lasting gift of joy and happiness.

The Editors
Harlequin Romance
225 Duncan Mill Road
Don Mills, Ontario, Canada
M3B 3K9

CHAPTER ONE

'MAY I help you?'

Her glasses had disappeared somewhere when she fell, and she had been fumbling around on the icy ground for their familiar shape when the deep voice with its thread of laughter interrupted her. She blinked upwards. Lord, he's big, was her first thought. Then she realised that the blurred figure was holding out a hand. Automatically her own reached out to clasp it and she was suddenly on her feet again with no apparent sign of effort on his part. She peered at her rescuer, feeling at a disadvantage. She hadn't recognised the voice and, even without her glasses, something told her that she would have remembered if she had ever met this man before.

'My glasses,' she muttered, looking vaguely around in the forlorn hope of distinguishing anything in the irritating blur that surrounded her without them.

'Here.' He put them in the hand he had just released.

She took them gratefully, ducking her head to put them on. 'Thanks,' she said with relief as the world came back into sharp focus. Then, remembering that he had also retrieved her from the slippery pavement, she added, 'Thanks for picking me up, too.' She smiled wryly up at him.

Her first impression hadn't been quite right. It was the bulky overcoat that had given her the impression of weight, but he was certainly tall. Definitely over six feet, she decided. That accounted for the ease with which he

had hoisted her own lanky frame back on its feet. She
dusted snow from her jeans while her rescuer seemed in
no hurry to move on.

'Are you all right?' he asked, that undercurrent of
amusement still in his voice. Briefly she wondered if he
was an actor.

'My dignity is a little brusied,' she admitted, accepting
from him the small parcel that had lain beside her. She felt
it anxiously and sighed with relief.

'Nothing else?'

So he *had* seen her sitting down hard in an untidy
sprawl, glasses flying as her feet skidded from under her.

'Nothing important,' she said as repressively as she
could, while resisting the temptation to brush the last
damp traces of snow from the offended area. He grinned,
unabashed. He had an infectious smile, she had to admit.
It challenged her to take offence and she found she
couldn't. She laughed. 'I mean it. You could carry me
home on a stretcher and Dad would merely frown over
the difficulties of manoeuvring it around the furniture,
but if I'd damaged that,' she indicated the parcel, 'then
the roof really would have fallen in.'

He lifted an eyebrow. 'What's in it? Fabergé eggs?'

'Not quite. It's an early Delft plate.'

Her father had lent it to a small exhibition at the local
museum, and she had been using her lunch break to
retrieve it. The reason for the force of her fall had been
the instinctive grasp she had kept on the parcel, instead of
trying to save herself. She had only put it down on the
ground when she began the hunt for her glasses. He was
looking intrigued. She saw that he recognised the value of
the plate. He probably has the same priorities as Dad, she
thought wryly, this time not hesitating to rub the

distinctly sore region of her anatomy. Her father thought she lacked commitment. She, however, merely claimed not to be obsessive.

He was chuckling again, but he was still interested. 'Your father collects Delftware?' he asked.

'And anything else that takes his fancy. It's selling it again that's the problem.' She thought of the overcrowded shop and the little flat above and behind it furnished with items he could not bear to part with. 'Just for a few months,' he would say as he brought in yet another bureau or chair.

The stranger was still looking curious, but she was frozen. She didn't have the advantage of an enormous and expensive overcoat to keep out the icy chill of a pallid January day. She looked at her watch. 'We run an antiques shop,' she finished her explanation, 'and it's due to reopen in five minutes, so I have to get back. Thanks again for salvaging the wreck.'

She gave him what she hoped was a cheerfully dismissive smile and turned to walk away. Unfortunately, she slipped.

A strong arm around her waist steadied her before she could once more make the ignominious descent to the pavement.

'*I'll* take the plate,' he told her. 'I prefer Delft in one piece, like your father, and I love antiques shops, so just lead the way. On second thoughts,' he amended, 'just give directions and we'll walk side by side. It's easier to catch you that way,' he explained. When she just stood there he reached out and calmly took the parcel from her, then took her hand in his and gave it a gentle tug. 'Come on. What are we waiting for?'

What indeed? This was absurd. Olivia Morris, twenty-three-year-old daughter of a local shopkeeper, walking hand in hand through the streets of her home Cotswold village where every third person would be wondering what she was up to. She tried to wriggle her fingers loose but he didn't seem to notice, and she didn't want to struggle too obviously. She'd probably fall over.

'It's about two hundred yards on our left,' she told him in resignation as they began walking.

Somehow her hand was still resting in his and, almost absently, he tucked it with his into the deep pocket of his coat. Since neither of them was wearing gloves, the sudden warmth was as welcome as it was unexpected. She gave him a startled glance but, as he didn't appear to notice, she decided that the return of feeling to her fingers was worth the odd sensation of intimacy. Especially as he seemed totally unaware of it.

She looked up at him again. Was he flirting with her? He had a strong, decisive profile, but his eyes were veiled by unusually long, dark lashes and she could read nothing in his expression except that constant lurking humour. She looked down at herself: faded jeans tucked into wellington boots and an old red anorak that was fraying at the cuffs. Her hair was bundled under a red woolly hat. No, she decided, there was no way this casually charming stranger was flirting with her. At first she had amused him; now he was on the trail of antiques and she was his friendly native guide. She wondered just how young the obsession started in people. Her father was over sixty, but this man didn't look more than thirty.

The shop was already open when they arrived at its door. Her father, an elderly-looking man, glanced up at the sound of the bell and smiled vaguely when he saw who it was.

'Did they give you the plate?' he asked at once.

'No trouble at the museum,' she told him, adding in a spirit of mischief, 'although I did fall over with it outside the chemist's. This gentleman rescued me.' She had repossessed her hand and now used it to indicate her companion. Her father, looking worried, ignored the gesture.

'Is it damaged?' he asked sharply.

'Not a chip,' said the man beside her, and handed over the parcel. The grin he gave her as her father carefully undid the wrappings to examine the plate was both conspiratorial and sympathetic.

Suddenly conscious of her sodden and dishevelled clothes, she infuriated herself by blushing.

'I must go and change,' she explained her hurried move to the rear of the shop. 'Thanks again for the rescue and escort. Do stay and browse if you want.'

This last advice was unnecessary. He was already opening the drawers of a Queen Anne tallboy and examining the grain. She decided to leave the men to it.

In the safety of her own room she stripped off not only the damp outer garments but also her jeans and shirt. They had both suffered from the snow. She did not waste much time deciding with what to replace them. Since she was old enough to understand what the words meant, she had heard, 'It's a pity she's such a plain child,' and had long ago accepted that dressing in fashionable or fussy clothes did nothing at all for what looks she had. She had grown to be above average height and thin, lacking the more obviously feminine curves she had often envied in her friends. Her face was full of planes and angles, the jawline too determined to be acceptable to most of the boys she had grown up with, the mouth too wide and mobile for conventional beauty. Her eyes, which she privately considered her best feature, were large and hazel, and she had always resented the trick of nature that forced her to hide them behind glasses. Contact lenses, however, turned her into a red-eyed and weeping hag within a few hours, so she had no choice.

She took a more respectable pair of jeans from the wardrobe, glad that at least she need never worry how trousers looked on her, and hesitated over her selection of a blouse. Just why she chose the turquoise silk that she normally wore only when she wanted to impress Jeremy she did not consider. It was a favourite shirt and it suited her, why justify it? She brushed out her long, curling chestnut hair and confined it in its usual loose ponytail at the nape of her neck. A touch of lipstick and mascara, and she was ready for the afternoon. As she brushed make-up on to her long lashes while squinting at her reflection in the mirror, she unexpectedly found herself remembering her rescuer's lashes. They were dark enough to need no colouring. How unfair that such an asset should be wasted on a man.

She returned to the shop, unsurprised to find the tall stranger still opening cupboards and turning plates upside-down to look at the mark. He had discarded his coat, putting a Victorian hat stand to its proper use, she noted, and was squatting in front of a rather dubious Jacobean cabinet, examining its elaborate decoration with a frown of disapproval. A pity, she thought. It had been one of her father's rare bad buys and was proving difficult to dispose of. It didn't seem likely to go to this man, either.

She thought she moved quietly, but he must have heard her since he rose at once and turned to her, his smile widening as though he liked what he saw. She had to grin in reply. After all, anything had to look better than she must have done earlier.

'Hello,' he said. 'Reporting for duty?'

'Something like that. Have you seen my father?'

'He went to look something up and fill in some papers. In his office, I think.'

She sighed. 'That leaves just me on call for the next hour,' she muttered, more to herself than to him.

'Suits me,' he said mildly, amused to see her blush again. That clear skin didn't hide much. 'I didn't expect to find such a treasure-trove when I stopped off here for lunch. In fact,' he added with that engaging smile, 'it makes up for lunch.'

'Why on earth did you pick this village of all places?' she wondered aloud.

With glasses no longer steamed up or blurry with snow, she was noticing more about him all the time. He was dressed casually in black trousers and a dark grey sweater, but it was quite obvious that neither came from any chain store, and the latter looked very like cashmere. She looked at his face clearly for the first time, and blinked. Her first instinct was that he was some sort of actor couldn't be far wrong. How on earth had she missed that stunning combination of dark blue eyes and black hair? She made a mental note to get her sight checked again as she took in his almost classically handsome features. Only that slight kink that spoke of a broken nose some time in his past marred their regularity, and it only gave distinction to what otherwise might have been cliché. Tall, dark and handsome—the conclusion was irrestistible, the reality even more so. He was certainly as tall as she had first thought, but his build was spare, and when he got up he had moved with the careless grace of the very fit.

Definitely an actor, she decided. His mobile eyebrow had too quickly noticed and commented on her survey, and laughter danced in his eyes at her reaction. Besides, somewhere she had seen that face before. It must have been on film.

'I read about it in a book,' he told her.

She was bewildered. 'About what?'

'Are you sure that fall didn't shake you up more than you said?' He was solicitous, but he was laughing at her. 'You asked me why I stopped here.' She vaguely remembered her earlier question and felt like a fool and, not unnaturally, thoroughly cross with him as a result.

'I'm perfectly all right,' she snapped, adding, 'What book?' He must think I'm some kind of moron, she thought wildly, beginning to feel hilarity rising in her. First I can't stand upright in the street, now I can't cope with the simplest of conversations.

He had propped himself on one corner of a refectory table and was observing her reactions as though she were providing some fascinating and totally unexpected entertainment.

'I was on my way from a job I was doing to my own home,' he at last explained. 'I'd read about the Crown Hotel here in a good food guide so I decided to stop for lunch.' She had no difficulty at all in interpreting his expression as he recalled his meal.

'Oh, dear,' she said in sympathy. 'I'm afraid it's changed hands since that guide was written.'

'Not an improvement?' he suggested.

She was fair. 'Only in some ways. It's not as crowded as it used to be.'

His lips twitched but he said, 'Understandably,' in

grave agreement. Then he went on, 'A damsel in distress and an excellent antiques shop more than compensate, however.' She was about to comment bluntly on this obvious hypocrisy when he added, 'I've made one or two purchases and I'll arrange transport in the next few days. Your father's got the details.'

'That's wonderful!' It was the best news she had had in weeks. Her father did not undervalue his stock, and there seemed to be less and less demand for high quality antiques in a remote Cotswold village. She kept most of the accounts and was all too aware of how much of their capital was tied up in the business and how slow the cashflow had become. She looked more benevolently on the visitor. 'Not the Jacobean cabinet, I suppose?'

'I'm afraid not. You're losing this table and the tallboy, and that small walnut desk.'

Loss. That was how her father would undoubtedly see it, but she was delighted. She could bring one or two things out of the flat and even improve the access to her own area of the shop.

'Good choice,' she acknowledged. 'And without this table in the way people might notice my side of things. I can even bring out a decent ladder.' She kicked the venerable oak legs without much respect.

'Ladder?' he queried.

She gestured to the almost inaccessible shelves behind him. 'We also deal in antiquarian books: they're my speciality, but it's a little difficult to get at the top shelf without room to fit in a set of library steps.'

His eyes had followed her gesture and he nodded. 'I see what you mean.' He looked back at her, 'Did you train as a librarian or an archivist?'

He sounded almost as though he was interested. The

very subject of old books seemed to bore most people, but since he couldn't go until her father had finished the paperwork he might as well have the serious answer he appeared to want.

She had told him in brief outline about her training in historical bibliography and book restoration, and been surprised by the sensitivity of his questions, when her father at last emerged from his office.

'Here you are,' he said, handing over some papers. 'You will take care of them, won't you?' He sounded almost ready to reject the sale if he had the wrong answer. Olivia held her breath. Customers had been known to back out at the last moment. This one didn't.

'I'll treasure them,' he said with apparent sincerity. Olivia saw her father relax as though reassured.

She reached out to retrieve the customer's coat from the rack. It was heavy and the quality was every bit as fine as she had expected. Why not? If he could afford to buy three very expensive pieces of antique furniture just because he was passing and liked them, he could certainly buy the best clothes available. At least he had good taste as well as money, she reflected as she handed over the coat.

He shrugged his long frame easily into it. 'Thanks,' he said, and seemed about to add something, probably about her tendency to fall over, when her father interrupted, ignoring as usual what anyone else was saying.

'Young Jeremy phoned while you were out,' he said. 'He wanted to know if you were free tonight and I said you were.'

She felt a familiar affectionate exasperation. She certainly had no other plans for tonight, but she did not appreciate her father's interference. She and Jeremy had been going out for a long time now, and there was a quiet understanding between them, but lately her father seemed to have been pushing her into something more definite, and it was beginning to make her feel obstinate.

Their customer was taking a card from his wallet, but he missed nothing of the conversation. He smiled slightly as though sympathising with her irritation.

'Boyfriend?' he assumed.

'Her fiancé,' said her father before she had a chance to reply.

An element of truth in this combined with her reluctance to begin a row in front of a stranger stoped her making the comment she wanted to. The stranger himself had looked surprised, glancing down at her ringless hands, but he made no direct comment when he next spoke. There was, however, a note of formality in his voice that she had not noticed before, and she sensed he was impatient to leave. I can't blame him, she thought. If he stays around, Dad will either try to interest him in something else or begin to complain about my unmarried state. Or both. Glad to be spared either prospect, she took the hand he held out to her, conscious of the strength in his fingers.

'Don't forget,' he was saying to her father, 'if you get in any of those items I mentioned, please contact me. You've got my card.' He turned to her. 'Goodbye, Miss Morris, it's been a pleasure meeting you. Take care of yourself, won't you?'

Circumstances, mainly the memory of herself sprawled on the pavement, stopped her from pointing out that she had been doing just that for as long as she could remember. She smiled sweetly, knowing he knew approximately what she would like to say, and murmured a polite goodbye, adding, 'Thank you for being such an excellent customer,' with considerably more sincerity.

'My pleasure.' He lifted a hand in farewell and was gone.

'Goodbye, Mr Courtenay,' said her father belatedly as the door closed.

It did not register at first, and then suddenly the name echoed in her mind. 'What did you call him?' she demanded.

'Mr Courtenay. It's his name,' he said, holding up a visitor's card as though explaining something to a child.

She took the card from him. Ross Courtenay. So *that* was why he knew so much about antiques, and was happy to spend several thousand pounds in an afternoon. She also realised exactly where she had seen him before, and it had nothing at all to do with films.

'Do you know him? I thought he was a stranger,' said her father as she stared at the card.

'He's certainly never been round here before.' For a moment she debated whether or not to explain. Her father was going to be disillusioned, and he had obviously liked their unexpected customer. She shrugged. He was bound to mention the name when he met other dealers, such large sales didn't come often, and someone was certainly going to tell him.

'He runs an organisation called Design House,' she told him. 'It's one of the most important, and select, firms of interior designers in the country.' Possibly also in Europe, but that was not really relevant.

The expression on her father's face might have been comic if she hadn't been saddened by it.

'You mean he wasn't buying for himself? That those pieces are going to people who can't even be bothered to choose their own furniture? But he said he'd treasure them,' he said plaintively. She soothed him.

'I'm sure he will. His work's very good and that's why people trust his judgement. I'm certain he wouldn't work anywhere where his efforts would be neglected or uncared for,' she tried to explain, a little indignant herself that Ross Courtenay had allowed them to assume he was a private customer. Then she smiled to herself; at least we didn't have to give him a trade discount, she realised.

'There was an article about him in a magazine I bought a few weeks ago,' she told her father. That was where she had seen him before, but the photograph had not conveyed the full impact of his appearance or the humour that had seemed to qualify his outlook on everything he encountered. 'I'll bring it down and show you, if I can find it.'

Her father didn't seem very interested, but when the shop closed for the day she went up to her room and found the magazine under a pile of books she had been working on. She looked around the room. It was her sanctuary: the only place in the cramped building where she could let her own choices dominate. In consequence it had little furniture and was light and airy despite its limited size. Much as she loved old things, she hated clutter even more, and preferred the two or three good pieces that she had to the crazy assortment of styles that had spilled over from the shop into the rest of their living accommodation. She closed the door and went to look for her father.

'Here's that article,' she told him.

Reluctantly he took the magazine. It was a glossy woman's journal and it evidently confirmed his worst fears about Mr Courtenay. 'I don't know why you waste your money on these things,' he said, flicking over the pages.

She didn't often, but it wasn't worth arguing about. She looked over his shoulder, memories of the item coming back as she read. It had begun as a general commentary on the rise of design consultants, and then had picked out Ross Courtenay as an outstanding example. He had started Design House only five years ago when he was twenty-five, and it seemed as though a combination of talent and sheer personality had made him successful, as well as highly fashionable. Now, the article suggested, he took only the work that interested him. While he was quite prepared to take on small and even unprofitable assignments from time to time, he flatly refused to expand the firm beyond its present size or to go into mass marketing. An interviewer had tried to provoke him by accusing him of snobbery.

'You can see it like that if you want,' the magazine quoted his reply, 'but I started out by using only my own tastes and values and, a bit later, those of a few colleagues I trusted. If I expand, that personal expertise will go and I'll get bored so quickly that I'll have to retire or start up something else and make my next million there.'

She could just imagine the interviewer's uncertainty about how seriously to take him. Oddly, she found herself believing he had spoken the plain truth, even though the journalist was clearly sceptical.

Her father shut the magazine. 'I still don't like the idea of asking someone else to choose your furniture,' he said stubbornly, and then, coming to the root of his dissatisfaction, 'and I do still think he ought to have explained why he was buying.'

Although she knew Ross Courtenay had been under no obligation to do so, Olivia couldn't help but share a little of her father's disappointment. The reticence seemed almost dishonest and didn't fit the image that their visitor had conveyed. In his own way he is an actor, after all, she reflected.

Her father stood up. He's looking old and tired, she thought with a sudden pang. His eccentricities might infuriate her at times, but they had been the only members of their family for a long time and there was a close, if undemonstrative, bond between them.

'Why don't I stay in and keep you company this evening?' she suggested. 'You can beat me at chess again and I'll see if I can find something exotic to cook for supper.'

He smiled at her but was obviously determined. 'You'll do no such thing. I think I feel more inclined to an omelette and an early night than one of your culinary experiments. Besides, you can't let Jeremy down.'

She saw no reason at all why she couldn't let Jeremy down, especially since she had had nothing to do with the evening's arrangements, but she accepted the insult to her good but individual cooking cheerfully enough and decided not to force the issue. The doorbell rang.

'That'll be Jeremy now. I'll go up and dress if you'll chat to him for a while.'

Before she went upstairs she opened the door to the familiar face of the man whom most of the village, including, usually, herself, assumed she would eventually marry. Jeremy Barker was three years older than herself and she found she was consciously noticing his appearance for the first time in months. He was about three inches taller than her own five foot seven and slim, his hair fair and his eyes a light blue. He had what she had always thought quietly attractive looks: a pleasant smile, neat features, and if his face lacked determination it also lacked aggression. He seldom tried to impose his ideas on her. He worked at the local bank and its respectable security suited him. She rarely saw him without a tie and suit. For a moment she felt a flicker of despair: life was so utterly predictable. Then the moment had passed and she was accepting his kiss on her cheek and standing back to let him in.

'I'm not quite ready yet,' she told him. 'Keep Dad company for a while, will you, while I do a speedy change? He can tell you all about our afternoon's customer.'

'Only one?' he teased.

'That's an improvement on some days—and this one didn't just browse.'

'Sounds promising.' Jeremy settled himself down opposite her father, automatically twitching the creases of his trousers as he did so. She wondered irrelevantly if he even owned a pair of jeans.

On reflection, she decided he probably didn't. She knew he disapproved of her wearing them for work, and she had had to convince him of their practicality.

'Skirts tend to sweep things off tables if you're not careful,' she had pointed out, 'and they can be very awkward up ladders.'

He had accepted her argument, but she knew his conventional soul still didn't like the idea. Perhaps, in fairness, it wsa the whole insecurity of the antiques business that worried him: it seemed too unreliable and unpredictable. She had to admit that there had been times lately when the vision he held out, of a world in which promotion and wage increases could be counted on as long as you followed the rules and worked hard, sounded very comfortable and attractive. If she married him she would never have to worry about balancing books or persuading customers to buy. Tonight, however, the prospect chilled her.

She shook her head. I must be getting a cold or something, she told herself. Depression just wasn't a normal part of her temperament. In a deliberate attempt to change

her mood she picked out a skirt that she knew Jeremy liked
and rejected the high heels she preferred in favour of shoes
that were almost flat. Jeremy tended to feel self-conscious
about the similarity in their heights.

He took her to a small Italian restaurant in a nearby town.
They dined there almost every week and were welcomed
with friendly smiles and an offer of their 'usual' table. The
food was good and they knew by now exactly what they liked
on the menu, so there was little discussion about ordering.

'You're looking very nice this evening,' he told her. 'Are
you celebrating your good fortune?'

She was puzzled for a moment. 'Good fortune?' Then she
understood. 'Oh, you mean Ross Courtenay's visit? Don't
tell me Dad didn't give you the full story of his duplicity?'
she chuckled.

He smiled indulgently. 'Of course he did. Anyone would
have thought he'd given you both a rubber cheque instead of
buying three of the most expensive items in the shop and
showing an interest in others. Don't forget, only last week
you were saying that no one seemed interested in antiques
any more. If I were you I'd try to keep in contact with your
Mr Courtenay—he obviously has the ideal outlet for your
more pricey stuff.'

'He's not "my" Mr Courtenay,' she protested
automatically. Still, she supposed he had a point. Common
sense told her she had every reason to celebrate this
afternoon's events. She lifted her glass. 'Here's to Mr
Courtenay's cheque-book,' she said, and grimaced slightly.

'What's wrong?' He was quick to notice her expression.
'Wine a bit sour? I must say, I didn't think this was quite as
good as our usual stuff. Let's abandon it and have a couple
of glasses of the regular plonk.' He summoned the waiter
and gave the order.

'I had a look at that bit in the magazine you showed your father,' he told her. 'Sounds as though Courtenay's done very nicely for himself: it's amazing what people will spend money on.' He was not mean, but Olivia knew he simply did not understand extravagance. 'Still, he's obviously a smooth talker if he managed to take your father in. I must say, I never can understand what people see in these pseudo-arty types. He's managed to make quite a profit at it, though,' he added with a hint of unwilling respect.

She was unexpectedly angry. She knew Jeremy's blind spots well enough and could usually ignore them, concentrating instead on his kindness and evident affection. Tonight, however, she had had enough. She didn't want to argue, so she feigned a yawn.

'I'm sorry,' she apologised. 'I'm afraid I'm not very good company this evening. Would you mind terribly if we skipped dessert for once and had an early night?'

'Of course not.' He glanced out of the window to where a few flakes of snow were beginning to flutter down in the light of a street-lamp. 'In fact, I was beginning to think we ought to start back: we don't want to risk being caught out by the weather.'

He drove carefully back through the dark roads, the thin new fall of snow crunching under the tyres. There were few lights on in the village, and when the car stopped outside the shop Olivia saw that her father's window was dark. He knows he can trust me with Jeremy, she thought with a combination of amusement and irritation. The sudden hush as the car's engine stopped made her aware of the silence of the streets, largely deserted despite the earliness of the hour. She undid her seat-belt, the click of Jeremy's sounding loud beside her. She turned to him and his arms came round her.

The taste of his lips on hers was familiar, reassuring, and

she clung to him for a moment with something like desperation. He was safe, and known, and loving. So why should she feel these surges of discontent? He responded to her unusual passion with eagerness and his hand was on her breast through the silk of her blouse when, the headlights of a passing car broke into their warm, dark world.

He drew back at once, sounding slightly embarrassed. 'I'm sorry, Olivia. It's too easy to get carried away with you. Look,' he added with sudden determination, 'why won't you agree to a formal engagement? We could easily afford to get married next year when my promotion comes though.'

She used the same excuse she always did. 'I don't see how I can leave Dad. He's not as strong as he pretends, and he can't possibly run the shop on his own.'

'But you could still help him out part-time when we're married, and by the time we could afford a family and you gave up work, he'd be retired. We could put an extension on the house so that he could live with us, if you liked,' he added persuasively. 'Besides, you know he wants to see you married.'

Whatever her private thoughts about the assumptions behind his earlier comments, she couldn't reject that last statement and she hesitated.

'Please, Livy,' he went on. 'We've known each other for over a year now—don't tell me you still need time. I know my feelings for you won't change.'

And nor, she feared, would her feelings for him. How did you make affection grow into love? Not that crazy passion that poets wrote about and which seemed to hurt so many people, she didn't expect to feel that, but the sort of caring on which you could reliably build a future? She had thought it would happen with time, but it hadn't. Now she wondered whether she shouldn't after all settle for what she did have,

and make both Jeremy and her father happy. It was no
good. Something deep in her rebelled at the dishonesty of
such a martyrdom. Even if it meant losing what she had,
she would still have to wait.

'I'm sorry, Jeremy,' she said at last, guessing that he
had already taken her silence as rejection. 'Give me a few
more months?' she coaxed.

He tried to tease her and she had to admire his lack of
anger. 'You think you'll be more willing in the spring? I'll
hold you to that. Now, you'd better go in or you'll freeze.
See you tomorrow?'

Nothing had changed. 'Fine,' she agreed, and leaned
over to kiss him quickly once again before slipping out of
the car and leaving him to drive home to the house he
shared with his parents.

She lay awake for some time that night, thinking about
her relationship with Jeremy. She wasn't sure any longer
that it had a future, and that certainly wasn't his fault.
She remembered the kiss in the car. It had been the need
for reassurance, not desire, that had moved her, she
realised, and fell asleep to the oddly disturbing knowledge
that her hand tucked within the warm grasp of a tall, blue-
eyed strange had stirred her more intimately than the
touch of Jeremy's hand upon her breast.

CHAPTER TWO

FIVE months later Olivia sat in her bedroom fingering a white visitor's card and reflecting on how drastically life could change. She had been crying, but the storm of weeping so idiotically triggered by the letter she had received in the afternoon post was over now. She felt drained.

For the past three months she had nursed her father, who had been paralysed by a stroke, opening the shop only occasionally just to stop him fretting. Then, a month ago, without further warning, he had died in his sleep, and now she was lost, hardly having the energy to do the many things that had to be done. She realised now why he had been pressuring her into marriage: he had known of the precarious state of his health for almost a year and had wanted to see her settled. It saddened her that he had died disappointed, but at least he had not known of Jeremy's engagement to Susan Turner. She smiled to herself and almost said aloud, 'Poor Jeremy,' as she recalled the way he had broken the news to her.

When her father had first become ill he had been most attentive and understanding, but she had so concentrated her emotions on her nursing duties that she had put all other relationships out of her mind. It had seemed at first as thought her father would recover, at least partially, and she began to adjust to the idea of caring for an invalid, perhaps for years. Unfortunately Jeremy had found it a prospect he could not deal with. At first she hardly noticed that he visited far less often, and then he had for once deliberately sought her out, looking embarrassed.

They had exchanged the usual greetings and he had enquired after her father and then there had been a pause.

'What's wrong?' she had asked, belatedly aware of his uneasiness.

'There's something I have to tell you, and I don't know how to do it,' he said eventually.

'As simply as possible,' she said. 'I'm so tired that I don't think I could face dramatics right now.' The strain of sitting up all night with her father made her speak more sharply than she intended, but at least it goaded him into replying.

'That's the trouble. I don't think you can face anyone or anything except your father.' He looked ashamed of himself but went on doggedly, 'I'm sorry, Livy, you're the last person in the world I'd want to hurt, but even before your father's illness you were so tied up with him and the business that I don't think I ever had your full attention.' She said nothing. Whatever her reasons, she knew he was right. 'Now, of course,' he continued, embarrassed but determined, 'you have no attention at all to spare for anyone else and you won't even try to share your problems. You did once say,' he reminded her, 'that I should give you until spring. Well, spring's half over now and I don't think you're any nearer loving me than you were in January, are you?' Before she could answer he had added the final blow. 'And even love can't survive for ever without some return.'

A note in his voice alerted her. 'And have you found someone who will return it?' she heard herself asking calmly.

His flush deepened and she saw his hands clench, but

he nodded. 'I think so. I've seen Susan Turner quite often, and she . . .'

Olivia stood up. 'Congratulations,' she told him. 'She's a splendid girl and she'll make you an excellent wife. I'm only sorry I've given you such a rotten time—don't worry,' she said, seeing the look on his face, 'you've nothing to feel guilty about. If anyone's behaved badly, it's me. Now, I've got to see to Dad, so I'll say goodbye.' She had kissed him quickly on the cheek and left the room before he could say anything else or see the sudden, unbidden tears that flooded her eyes.

It wasn't a lost love she was crying for, she knew that, and in some ways her immediate life would be simpler without him, it was just the sense of increasing isolation that momentarily overwhelmed her.

Over the next few months, she had found little time to spare for thoughts of the future, but her father's death had forced her to face the stark reality of her situation. Once the funeral was over she had begun to assess the state of the business: it was at least as bad as she had feared. It had always been precarious, but the months of inattention had left the finances of the shop little short of catastrophic. To meet the debts most of the stock would have to be sold quickly, and it certainly wouldn't realise enough capital for her to re-start any sort of business. She would have to look outside the village for work, since there was no chance of anyone local wanting a specialist in antiquarian books. That meant selling the shop itself and moving to a city. Even then she might not have enough money to buy even a small flat, and she suspected that jobs in her line did not come up frequently. Belatedly she wished she had taken up the secretarial course she had once rejected with impatience. Her restricted skills now did not seem very marketable.

Selling the stock had proved even more difficult then she had feared. Agents had constantly tried to undercut her prices, arguing that they knew better than 'a young girl who's only seen a little of the business.' For all she knew there could have been some truth in their comments, but she couldn't afford to drop the prices too far.

Finally, wearied by grief and the struggle to salvage something from the ruins of the business, she lost patience and decided to auction everything, house and stock, and simply accept whatever meagre profit she made once the debts were cleared. Having made that decision she had at once felt better, glad that something was settled, and had turned with more resolution to the task of sorting and tidying the last of her father's things. It was then that she had come across Ross Courtenay's visiting card.

She had sat and looked at it for some time, surprised that it had not been thrown away. She remembered vividly that day they had met: even thinking about it made the late spring sun outside seem inappropriate to that icy afternoon and early January chill. She thought of his words to her father about contacting him if he found any interesting pieces. Naturally her father would never have contacted someone he mistrusted, but was that any reason why she shouldn't? She had looked around the shop again with new eyes. The goods were as high quality as ever: perhaps an auction was not the only solution.

And so, last week, she had written a short letter to the address handwritten in black on the back of the card. She had not mentioned her father's death, only that they had several pieces that might interest him if he liked to make contact. He would wonder why she wrote and not her father, but she did not want the letter to sound like a plea for charity. If he came, she could explain then.

It was only when the letter had arrived that afternoon that she had realised just how much she had counted on his interest. She had not realised who it was from at first. The envelope was typed, not written in that decisive black scrawl on the back of the card. Then she read the equally formal letter. It was not from Ross Courtenay, it was from his secretary. Mr Courtenay, it seemed, was 'unavailable'. The letter thanked her for her information and said it would be passed on at the first opportunity. Olivia didn't believe a word of it. She and the shop had amused him for an afternoon, but he had no need to look for antiques in obscure country villages that were far from anywhere.

She had cried then until the self-mockery that she used to control her feelings returned. 'Why on earth *should* he remember you?' she asked herself. 'He lives in a completely different world from people like you and it's about time you admitted it.' It wasn't the first time she had silently acknowledged that her hope of seeing Ross Courtenay again wasn't just as a solution to her financial crisis.

She had crumpled the letter and thrown it into the waste-paper basket, and was wondering whether to do the same with his card when she heard the bell that told her someone was in the shop.

'Blast!' She got to her feet, hoping her eyes didn't betray her tears too obviously and cursing her decision to open the shop that day. She thought of leaving the unwanted customer to browse and disappear without her attention, but there were too many small and valuable objects around to take that risk. She emerged from the

flat into the dimmer light of the shop, and promptly
tripped over a Victorian footstool that she had moved
earlier and forgotten about.

She was caught and held against a broad male chest,
strong arms steadying her and a voice above her head
quivering with amusement.

'How on earth have you managed to stay in one piece
since I last saw you?' asked Ross Courtenay.

The fine cotton of his shirt was warm under her cheek,
and she knew a moment's insane longing to put her arms
around his waist and just lean on him. But of course that
was impossible. And then he was stepping back and
tipping up her chin with his long fingers so that he could
look down at her. At once all trace of humour left his face,
concern showing in the dark blue eyes.

'But you aren't in one piece, are you?' he demanded
quietly. 'Are you going to tell me about it?'

Behind the lenses of her glasses she felt her eyes fill. She
sniffed. 'It's not your problem,' she managed to mutter.

'Isn't it?' he mused. He looked around the shop, seeing
that he was again the only customer. 'Look, why don't
you declare an early-closing day and then I can tell you all
my problems as a sort of swap? You can even show me the
furniture you mentioned in your letter if you want to: at
least *that* is my business. Even if this isn't,' he added
softly, reaching out to touch the one tear that had escaped
and trickled down her cheek.

Shaken by the unexpectedly tender gesture, she almost
lost control. She turned away. 'OK,' she said, her voice
husky. 'You put up the ''closed'' sign and bolt the door,
and I'll make some coffee. Come on through to the living-
room.'

The familiar task restored her control. When she

brought the tray through from the kitchen she no longer felt the urge to howl out all her troubles. And how that would have appalled him, she thought, arrested by the sight of the long-legged figure she remembered so vividly sprawled in one of the room's several armchairs. He looked so improbable, and so at home, that she wondered for a moment whether she had conjured him up from her own exhausted dreams. Her lips twitched at the image of him as a benevolent, if slightly flippant, genie from the sort of little brass lamp her father refused to have in the shop.'

He caught the flickering expression and smiled as he came easily to his feet and took the tray from her.

'That's better. Come and sit down and let me tell you about the two weeks I've just spent in America and the truly awful things a rather nice Texan family wanted me to do to their home.'

'So you really were unavailable?' The question slipped out before she could stop it.

'Did you doubt it?' She did not trust the sorrowful expression a bit. His eyebrows lifted in mockery as he asked, 'Just what did you do with Miss Johnson's elegant letter?' Then, seeing her blush, he added with uncomfortable acuity, '*Don't* tell me you thought it was all a polite lie and threw it away? Really, Olivia,' he ended with a reproachful look.

Embarrassed as well as amused, she could only ask, 'Who's Miss Johnson?'

He leaned back in his chair. 'Who indeed? What sort of secretary, I wonder, do you imagine I have?' He glanced ceilingwards as though searching for inspiration. 'Blonde? Beautiful? Curvaceous?' He sketched a graphic outline with eloquent hands and smiled at her ready colour. 'Shame on you. Miss Johnson, perish the thought, is old enough to be my mother, well-corseted, grey-haired and *very* efficient. She is also a firm believer in the old-fashioned virtues, such as formality in letter-writing, and is determined to protect me from being pestered. Even when I'd love to be pestered,' he added sorrowfully. 'Anyway,' he went on, 'she's also remarkably conscientious, so she did as she promised and showed me your letter yesterday when I got back from the States.'

'You acted on it very promptly,' she said, impressed. His light tone had let her relax and she felt more at ease with him now. 'You must be as conscientious as Miss Johnson.'

'Abosultely,' he gushed with elaborate insincerity, then grinned. 'But don't bank on my having the same regard for such things as old-fashioned virtue.'

'Do you *enjoy* watching me blush?' she demanded, seeing the glint in his eyes.

'I love it,' he admitted. 'Are you going to do it again?'

'Not if I can help it,' she told him firmly, and smiled at his appreciative chuckle.

A sort of companionable quiet settled between them. For someone so obviously full of vitality and energy, he was surprisingly comfortable to be with. She discovered that she felt better than she had in weeks. It must be because he makes me laugh, she decided, and wondered when she had last felt like laughing. She could hardly remember, and even now laughter, however heartening, seemed incongruous.

He saw the shadow on her face and when he spoke again his voice was serious. 'Has something happened to your father? Is that what's wrong?'

She was glad of his quick observation and deduction. It made the explanation easy, after all. 'He died last month,' she said simply.

'I'm sorry. I only met him once, but I liked him.' She believed him, but the memory of that one meeting brought a moment's anger as she recalled her father's hurt.

'He liked you,' she said, resentment showing, 'until he realised that the things you bought were for other people.' She shrugged. 'Oh, I know it's silly, and no real concern of his, but he liked your taste and thought you were choosing things to live with, not to furnish other people's houses.'

He looked astonished. 'But that's exactly what I was doing. If it had been a firm's transaction I'd have told him so—he was obviously concerned about what would happen to the pieces. Didn't you hear me say I'd look after them?'

She felt like an idiot, and ashamed. 'Yes, but——'

'But you thought the playboy designer was just being facile?' There was a hint of disappointment, almost of bitterness, in his voice.

'I'm sorry, I should have known better.'

He looked severe for a moment, but then smiled quite gently. 'You should indeed, but I'll forgive you this time. Now,' he went on more briskly, 'how do you want me to help you?'

He sounded ready to turn his hand to anything, and she knew a wild impulse to say, 'Take over.' He'd run a mile, she decided, and began to explain her situation.

'So you see,' she finished at last, 'I have to dispose of everything, and I thought you might be interested in some of it before I put the rest up for auction. I'm afraid,' she admitted, 'Dad didn't keep the list you gave him of what you were interested in, and, of course, if there's nothing here that you want, then there's no real obligation at all. I'm very grateful to you for coming, anyway,' she added, with more feeling than she intended.

He said nothing at first, a small frown on his forehead, and her heart sank. 'I'll tell you what I'll do,' he said at last. 'I'll have a good look round just to see what you've got and then we can talk about it. I've an idea, but you might not agree to it, so let's see what there is to start with, OK?'

'Sounds fine,' she agreed. 'Do you want me to show you round or would you rather explore on your own?'

'On my own, if you don't mind. But don't go too far away: I might feel lonely, or in need of expert advice.'

'I wouldn't trust my advice if I were you. Books are my speciality, remember? Besides,' she grinned, 'I'm not like my father—I don't mind lying in the interests of making a sale.'

'You shock me,' he said without apparent concern. 'Now I won't even be able to consult you about the books.'

'If you'll take that blasted Jacobean cabinet I'll be honest about the rest,' she offered.

He winced, then pretended to give the matter some thought. 'I might be able to palm it off on the Texans, I suppose.' Then he shuddered. 'No, think of my reputation and ask for anything else.'

'That, or nothing,' she said firmly, and went into the study, leaving him to browse as he wished. Her general knowledge of antiques was, in fact, good, but she suspected there was little she could tell him.

He took well over an hour and did actually ask her once

or twice about the provenance of a piece, and she saw that he had made full notes. He really was taking this seriously, she realised with pleased surprise. At last he rejoined her in the living-room.

'Now at least I've some notion of what you're dealing with,' he told her. 'Your father had quite an eye for quality, didn't he? It's a pity he didn't have an outlet in a major town somewhere. Not that I mean to insult this village's charm,' he added.

'Don't worry, I agree with you. But Dad hated towns. Let's face it, he was born to be an eccentric collector with unlimited private funds, not a salesman.' She smiled ruefully.

'I wish I'd met him earlier.' So did she, but there was no point in saying so. He surveyed the room. 'He liked to live with his stock, didn't he?

'Definitely. Have a look around. I'd prefer to hang on to the bits in my bedroom if possible, but basically it's all got to go. Go on,' she urged, seeing his curiosity, 'have a prowl.' Some of the best pieces were in the flat, and she was beginning to hope he might buy several items.'

He returned quite shortly, looking thoughtful, but the ready humour was soon back. 'I took the opportunity of exploring your room too,' he admitted without apology. 'I see why you want to keep that sofa table and the nursing chair. Wouldn't your father let you have anything else?' he teased her about the room's relative emptiness.

'I practically had to bar the door to keep the furniture out,' she admitted.

'You've got good taste. Too many people like you around and I'd be out of a job.'

It was an easy compliment, probably paid a hundred

times, but she was idiotically pleased.

He had been watching her, smiling sometimes as the life came back into her face, although she still looked drawn. Now he looked at her hands. There was still no sign of a ring, and that both pleased and puzzled him.

'What's happened to your fiancé?' he asked, deceptively offhand. 'Jeremy, wasn't it?'

'It was,' she agreed. 'Though the engagement was never very formal. He's going to marry the proverbial girl-next-door. *Much* more suitable: she's pretty and at least outwardly biddable, and even in high heels she isn't much taller than his shoulders,' she said cheerfully.

'Oh. Are you being very noble and brave?'

'Not really,' she shrugged.'

'Not even slightly broken-hearted?' he suggested.

She considered. Well, I did cry when he told me—after he'd gone—but I think that was more a sort of general depression,' she said honestly.

'Good.' He looked pleased. 'Depression's much easier to sort out.'

She couldn't help smiling. 'Why on earth should you want to?'

'Philanthropy?' he offered, and was rewarded by an expressively disbelieving snort of laughter. 'I see I'll have to convince you, but possibly that had better wait for some other time. Aren't you impatient to hear what I've got to say about your stock?'

'Breathless,' she told him, not really joking

'Right. As I said earlier, it's almost all of very fine quality, and I think you're running the risk of losing a great deal of its value if you put it up for auction as a single sale. Especially a country auction. If word gets round, the professionals will be down like the sharks they resemble. I don't know much about your books,' he added slowly, 'but I suspect much the same would be true of them.'

'It's what I feared,' she agreed, disappointed but unsurprised. 'It just seemed like the only way of solving the problem quickly.'

'I can see that.' He was unusually serious. 'I do have an alternative suggestion if you're interested.'

'I'll listen to anything,' she said willingly.

'Careful. I might remind you of that one day. What I was going to say was that you could sell the flat and shop premises independently and I could agree a valuation on all the contents with you. Then I could buy the whole lot and re-sell the items I don't want at my own convenience and where I know they'll go best.' He looked at the stunned expression on her face. 'Don't worry,' she heard him say, 'I don't need an answer at once and I really will give you a fair price—and not lose out myself on the deal.'

'Are you serious?' She couldn't believe it.

'For once, yes. It's good business, I assure you.' He seemed so anxious to convince her of his mercenary motives that she at once doubted him.

'This isn't some sort of charity?' she persisted.

'Good heavens, no!' He sounded horrified at the idea. 'I think you've grown so used to living with all this around you,' his gesture included the contents of the flat and the shop, 'that you've never stopped to think about its quality. I'd be mad if I let the opportunity pass—it's you who's doing me the favour, you know.'

She didn't know anything of the sort, but she wasn't going to argue further. 'All right, I surrender. Send in your valuers and we can argue about the relative merits of Hepplewhite and Chippendale.'

'In my business you accept either, thankfully, the moment they cross your path, and don't argue about the cost. The customer,' he added blandly, 'can always afford it.'

'Lucky him,' she said with feeling. She looked at the man who seemed able to solve her problems effortlessly. 'You do realise you've just deprived me of my current major preoccupation?' His lifted eyebrows asked the question she answered. 'Worrying about how on earth I was going to cope with sorting everything out. If I put the flat and shop through the local estate agent I've probably got a few months at least to find a job and somewhere to live. And that's never seemed such a daunting prospect as the rest.'

Something in his expression stopped her. He was, she thought, watching her as though trying to calculate her reaction to some unknown situation. There was a smile lurking in those midnight eyes, and a reckless look as though he was about to gamble on some outside chance, and still expected to win. When he spoke there was a hint of challenge in his voice.

'What would you say if I offered you a solution to that problem, too?'

She was silent for a moment. She wondered briefly what he would do if she flung her arms around his neck and hugged him. Wisely, she did no such thing; she doubted if she would know how to cope with either polite rejection or enthusiastic response.

'I thought earlier that you looked like some sort of genie from a magic lamp; now I'm certain of it. Do you reorganise the life of every girl you pick up?' she asked instead.

'Only those who fall over three times,' he told her

gravely. 'And you fell twice in the snow—nearly—and once this afternoon. It's a far more potent spell than brass polish and a muttered "abracadabra",' he assured her.

'I'm almost willing to believe it. Dare I ask what this solution is that you've come up with?' Somehow it seemed important to resist the temptation to let him take over her life completely.

'Of course.' He nodded. 'I've got to give you a little family history first so that you'll understand the situation, but I'll try not to bore you.' She was fascinated. 'Until last year I lived fairly contentedly in a London flat: it's comfortable and convenient and I'm not going to get rid of it, but I began to wonder about getting somewhere in the country as well. Somewhere that could be a real home but was big enough to work from too. And then, fortuitously, my Uncle Hubert died last November.'

'Fortuitously?'

'Well, he wasn't much loss as an individual. He managed to loathe almost everyone he met and he only left the house to me because I was the only relative who never bothered him.'

'Clever of you.'

He shuddered. 'I avoided him like the plague. I was dragged along twice on duty visits when I was a child and I was terrified on both occasions.' She somehow couldn't imagine it. 'But even then,' he added, 'I loved the house. Or parts of it—the bits that didn't have ferocious animal heads stuck to the walls.'

'So you've acquired a house plus the remnants of several endangered species. I still don't see where I come in.'

'You will, and I expect most of the species are already extinct if Uncle Hubert had anything to do with it. I've disposed of those, plus most of the other horrors in the house. His taste in furniture,' he explained, 'matched his taste in wall hangings. I've begun the refurbishing, and in fact you should recognise at least three of the pieces I've installed.' His look reminded her of her earlier error.

'I've already apologised,' she protested.

'I should hope so. Anyway,' he went on, 'what I was coming to was the one room in the house I can't quite decide what to do with, and I haven't anyone in the firm who can cope, either. The library.' He looked for her reaction, but she was very cautious.

'You must be able to find experts in any subject without trouble. Why ask me? I might not be any more able to cope than your staff.'

'If you're not, then I'll just have to learn from my mistakes, but if you don't have your father's obsessions I'm damned sure you do have his integrity and knowledge of your subject.' He seemed to be as aware as she was of his uncharacteristic intensity and relaxed. 'Besides, you're far better-looking than most experts.'

This patent lie made her laugh, especially when she saw his pained expression. 'All right, you've inherited a library. Why do you need help with it?'

'Because, from what I can tell, it contains an odd selection of books. Some seem quite unusual to me, some need attention, some are utter junk—and I've not the faintest idea how to distinguish between them, organise them or restore them. I don't want just a display collection of similarly bound books, you know. I like books I can read, and if there's anything of real value it might be better off in a museum.' He smiled suddenly, coaxing and challenging. 'You are going to do it, aren't you?'

She was helpless. 'It sounds wonderful,' she had to admit, 'and it'll give me longer to find something permanent.' Then she frowned. 'But I've no idea where you—or Uncle Hubert—live.' The address she had written to had been in London. 'How can I commute from here to——'

He interrupted, the expression on his face resembling a child caught out in mischief. 'I knew you'd find the snag eventually,' he said. 'The Grange is in Wiltshire, about three hours' drive from here. I'm afraid you're going to have to come and live in Uncle Bluebeard's castle for a month or so.'

'With you?' What was there about this man that reduced her conversation to imbecility? His grin was wicked.

'With me, with my secretary, the cook, the gardener, with various people who work for me, including Patrick Sayers, who's been trying to tidy books and is beginning to choke on the dust and will obviously adore you, not to mention sundry itinerant guests, and probably even my sister who lives about ten miles away,' he finished without apparent need for breath. 'Have I managed to put you off entirely?'

She had begun to laugh. 'No, you've just sold it to me completely. When do I start?'

'No quibble about wages?'

'The man saves me from my creditors, gives me a job and a roof over my head, and now he wants to *pay* me?' she asked a fat china Buddha who sat on top of a nearby bookcase.

'The labourer is worthy etc.,' he reminded her piously.

'Yes, well, you'd better check the quality of my labour

first,' she said frankly, and then added, 'and let me thank you. A few hours ago I was as near to giving up as I'd ever been, and now you've managed to find answers to a series of apparently insoluble problems. You've got to accept a little gratitude.'

'I don't want it.' His voice was flat.

'Too bad. It's yours, I'm afraid.'

He seemed about to protest again, but then something changed his mind. He stretched in his chair and yawned. 'Are you *really* grateful?' he asked.

'Of course. Why?' Suspicion edged her voice and he smiled.

'It's just that my stomach doesn't know if it's in Dallas or London, but it thinks it's time for a meal. Could you bear my company somewhere?'

She grinned. 'The Crown?'

'I think I've just lost my appetite,' he decided.

She thought briefly of the Italian restaurant that she and Jeremy used to visit, and then said, 'I've got a better idea. Why don't you stay put and let me cook for you? It's the least I can do, and I can promise you won't die of food poisoning.'

'It sounds wonderful. Infinitely superior to the Crown. You mean I just have to sit here and let myself be waited on?'

'You may have to open the wine.'

'Slave-driver. All right. Bring it on.'

Between teasing and laughter and some lively opinions about antiques and design in general, they shared the excellent meal that Olivia made from the odd assortment of food in the refrigerator, and a bottle of good wine. She had bought it once to share with Jeremy, but they had never opened it, since he preferred red to white.

The evening was almost over and he was grumbling about the drive ahead of him, having declined her offer of the spare room, when she decided she had to ask the question that had come back to her again and again. His attention seemed a long way away. She hesitated.

'Mr Courtenay,' she began, and he laughed.

'Are you trying to put me in my place? You may not have noticed, but I have been calling you Olivia since just after you fell over that stool. I agree it's about time you called me something,' so he had noticed her careful evasions, 'but I think Ross would be much nicer. It's Miss Johnson, not me, who likes formality, remember?'

'All right,' she said, determined, 'Ross. Will you be serious for one moment and explain why you're doing all this for me?'

'More philanthropy?' he suggested.

She restrained the rude comment that sprang to her mind. 'Not good enough.'

He sighed and looked at her. The long lashes half veiled the dark blue eyes so that she could not read them, then they opened fully and she still saw nothing beyond that flicker of entertainment and hidden mirth.

'It's just that it's going to be so much easier to seduce you if we're living together,' he said simply, and waited for her reaction.

CHAPTER THREE

SITTING on a train that wound its way through the Wiltshire countryside, Olivia remembered that comment and smiled. For a moment she had been completely stunned, and then the absurdity of it, coupled with his expectant look, had sent her into almost uncontrollable laughter. When she recovered enough to wipe her eyes and look at him, he was watching her with an amused smile.

'I think I ought to be deeply wounded by that response,' he observed.

'I'm sorry,' she managed, still fighting the urge to giggle, 'but you shouldn't say things like that in answer to serious questions.'

'It's the only answer you're going to get,' he had told her, and then he had stood up. 'I must go. I'll be in contact tomorrow or the next day, but shall we provisionally plan for you to come down to Wiltshire in about two weeks?'

And so she had spent the past fortnight packing up and labelling for storage the things she wanted to keep, and creating what order she could in the crowded building. They had decided that it should go on the market only after the contents had been cleared, so all she had to do was pack a bag and lock the door behind her.

She gave the key to Jeremy. It was not a gesture intended to irritate Susan Turner, although she was unworried by the suspicion that it would have that effect,

44

but he was someone she knew who would be utterly reliable and conscientious about keeping an eye on her old home. In fact, he seemed quite pleased by the responsibility, as though it relieved him of some of the guilt he felt about ending their relationship, and reassured him that she bore him no grudge. It was clear, however, that he did not wholly approve of her new job.

'Isn't it taking a bit of a risk?' he had asked anxiously. 'After all, you don't really know what this fellow Courtenay's like, and going off to some remote country house isn't the same as taking a proper job somewhere, is it?'

Amused as well as annoyed, she had said, 'I've either got to trust him or risk ending up in debt.' She had known he would wince at that thought. 'Besides, if working for Ross Courtenay, however temporarily, isn't a "proper" job, then I can't think what might be. His reputation isn't built on hot air, you know.' Jeremy's expression of doubt made her want to giggle and she wished that Ross could see it. 'Don't worry, you've got the address and phone number so you can always call in and check up on me if you feel the need. Susan might not like it, though,' she added thoughtfully.

'Sue understands that I'm bound to feel concern for someone in your position,' he said stiffly, and she wondered just how well he knew the girl he intended to marry.

He had gone away looking only a little more satisfied, and she wondered what he would have said if he had known just how complicated her feelings about the future really were. The thought of the coming weeks exhilarated and terrified her. Her life so far had been fairly confined, and she had certainly never met anyone like Ross before.

She doubted if there were many people like him: assured
and successful, flamboyant and irreverent, but with that
unexpected streak of sensitivity that could be so
disconcerting. Professionally this job was going to be a
challenge, but concern about that occupied her far less
than thoughts of her personal reaction to her employer.

He had teased her and provoked her. But, after her first
startled laughter at his parting comment, she had found
his words coming back to her and had been all too aware
of the attraction this man and his easy charm could hold
for her if she let them. The last thing she must allow
herself to do, she realised, was to take his flirting
seriously. It was probably second nature to him and,
besides, hadn't he already agreed that he liked to make
her blush? If thoughts of his long-legged casual elegance
and expressive blue eyes occurred too often for her
comfort, that was no reason to let anyone else know of
them.

She woke from her reverie and stared out of the window
as the train jolted into a station. She peered at its name.
The next stop was the one she wanted. She glanced at her
watch. Twenty minutes to go. Nervous butterflies
crawled in her stomach. Perhaps she should have dressed
more formally? She had a skirt in her bag that she could
easily change into. Nonsense, she told herself. You've
worn jeans every time he's seen you, he probably doesn't
know you've got any other clothes, and if you do change
he might think you're trying to impress him. She sat back
in her seat as the train started again. He might not even
be there. He had said when they'd last spoken on the
phone that he was spending a lot of time in London, but
that he would make sure someone met her.

Who? The formal secretary? The gardener? Most

likely the gardener, she decided, and half hoped Ross would be in London. It might be easier to fit into her new surroundings without his unnerving presence.

The last miles passed quickly, and then they were at the station and she was turning the stiff lever that opened the door. It swung wide and, before she could make another move, a hand had reached down to pick up her heavy suitcase.

'What have you got in here? Tablets of stone?' Ross asked as he feigned injury.

She pushed the glasses back up the bridge of her nose, a defensive gesture she had long used to hide her reactions.

'One or two textbooks,' she admitted as she took the long step down to the platform.

He didn't offer to help, instead he said, 'You didn't fall over,' sounding mildly disappointed.

'I've been practising,' she told him confidentially. 'I can walk quite well now.'

'Pity. I rather enjoyed catching you. Oh, well, I suppose it's time I took you off to my den of vice.' He saw her reaction and at once demanded, 'What's funny?'

She chuckled. 'Nothing much, except that that's approximately where Jeremy thinks I'm going. Not that he said so explicitly, of course.'

'Oh, does he? So you've told him where you'll be?' His voice held only casual interest.

'I had to. I left him, so to speak, minding the store.' She explained about the keys.

'I see. Come on, then, the car's out this way.' He lifted her case without apparent effort and headed rather fast for the station entrance.

She followed him, reminding herself that he was now her employer as well as her rescuer, and she had to expect some change in their relationship.

When she caught up he was standing outside a battered Land Rover, her case already in the back. He must have read her expression accurately.

'Don't worry. I have something altogether flashier for London. Around here, however, this is the only practical transport.'

Whatever had momentarily irritated him seemed to have passed. He held the door open for her and made no secret of watching her long legs as she stepped up into the mud-spattered vehicle. She said nothing, but was glad she had resisted that impulse to wear a skirt.

The drive to the house took about twenty minutes, and the last part was up an unpaved and rutted track that explained the state of the Land Rover.

'Your uncle didn't exactly encourage visitors, did he?' she said as the car lurched sideways across an unexpected pot-hole.

His hands hardly tightened on the wheel as he steered around the worst craters. 'We've removed most of the mantraps and filled in the bear-pit,' he reassured her. 'Mere details like resurfacing the drive will take another month or two.'

She hadn't known quite what to expect of his house. Georgian elegance had somehow seemed most appropriate, so she was totally unprepared for what she saw. She supposed there might once have been a neatly symmetrical little eighteenth-century house on the site, but some later owner had clearly had extravagant ideas and the money with which to indulge them. Two wings had been added to the original building. One was fantastically castellated, the other ended in an absurd circular tower with a short conical spire. The whole effect was somehow both ludicrous and delightful, the slightly weathered whitewash and ancient spread of wisteria giving the house a unity it could not otherwise possibly have possessed.

She could not help it. She laughed aloud. His profile didn't turn towards her as he negotiated the cattle grid that presumably indicated the main gate, but she saw his lips twitch responsively and guessed that he was not offended by her response.

'It has been called a monstrosity,' he admitted as they drew up at the elaborate steps leading to the front door.

'It's marvellous,' she protested. 'It's got such character, and for some crazy reason, it fits in absolutely with its surroundings.' It was true. The odd house should have looked uncomfortably out of place in the woodland and lawns around it, but somehow it was completely right.

'It does, doesn't it?' he agreed. 'I told you I loved it. Come on in and meet whoever's around. You're under no obligation to be as enthusiastic about all of them as you are about the house,' he added as he opened her door.

At the top of the steps was a figure she had no trouble in identifying as Miss Johnson even before he introduced her. She was greeted quite formally and had the feeling that the middle-aged woman was reserving judgement as she said, 'I'm pleased to meet you, Miss Morris.' Olivia felt uncomfortably that the jeans had counted against her, especially in comparison with the secretary's neat blue suit.

Behind her, Ross put down the heavy suitcase. 'I'll get someone to take that up for you later. Come on into the living-room and meet whoever's there.'

He led the way into a spacious, lofty room that must

have been part of the original house. In front of the Adam fireplace were two people and, although they fell silent as the door opened, she felt certain they had been arguing. Ross took in the situation without comment. He gestured to Olivia and spoke impartially to both the man and the woman.

'This is Olivia. She tends to fall over, but she's thoroughly house-trained and she doesn't break things.' Did she imagine a glance flickering at the woman? 'She's also,' he added, 'very good with books. Old ones.'

The fair young man heaved an extravagant sigh of relief and shook her hand. 'Thank goodness for that!' He smiled engagingly at her. 'I'm Patrick Sayers and I've been trying, among a million other things, to find out what's in that barn of a room, with a reference book in each hand and dust-clogged lungs, ever since we came down here. The place is an utter mess, and if I wasn't almost as selfish as Ross I'd warn you off it.'

'But you are, so you won't,' interrupted their employer. 'Olivia, meet Theresa Stanley, who seems to be the only other resident at the moment. She's the needlepoint and fabric expert.'

Olivia took the hand that was offered, but could see no welcome in the other woman's pale blue eyes. It's a pity about the coldness, she found herself thinking; she's got everything else it takes. She could see no flaw in the petite and very feminine figure. And then the woman had turned to Ross and any hint of chill had vanished.

'Ross,' she exclaimed, a small hand reaching out to touch his sleeve, 'couldn't you spare me just a couple of hours this afternoon? I desperately need your advice about the designs for Lady Rushton's curtains.'

'It'll have to wait, I'm afraid,' he said with

apparent regret. 'Now Olivia's safely here I've got to go
up to London. I should be back some time tomorrow
afternoon and we can sort it out then.' He looked at
Olivia. 'Sorry to desert you so soon. The truth, of course,
is that I can't face your reaction when you actually see
what you've taken on. I'll leave you in Patrick's care.
Don't bully him, and try not to fall off any ladders, won't
you?' He had somehow taken her hand as though in
conventional farewell, but before she could realise what
he was up to he had lifted it and touched it fleetingly to his
lips in a gesture that left her speechless. He didn't seem to
expect a response, however, and raised his hand in
general farewell to the others before leaving the room with
the deceptively casual decisiveness that she was beginning
to recognise.

She turned from watching his disappearance, feeling
unexpectedly bereft, to the other two people in the room.
Theresa was looking distinctly cross and Patrick had a
speculative gleam in his eye that did not reassure her at
all.

There was an uncomfortable silence, and then Patrick
smiled wryly. 'Welcome to The Folly,' he said. She
looked a question. 'It's what most people call this place
once they've seen it,' he explained, 'but I sometimes
wonder if it doesn't say something about the inhabitants,
too. Do you feel strong enough for the guided tour?'

'I'd love it.' And it would get her away from Theresa's
irrational hostility.

An hour later she was wondering whether she would
ever find her way round the extraordinary maze that
rebuilding had make of the house's internal structure.
Patrick, however, was altogether more straightforward
than the building. He was only a couple of years older

than herself and, beneath the manner that she suspected
he sometimes adopted in half-conscious imitation of Ross,
she discovered someone very willing to be friendly and
completely devoted to his employer.

'I joined him for some part-time work experience when
I left art college,' he told her. 'I think he must have
admired my nerve in asking for the job or something.
Anyway, I'm still here. He claims to be training me up to
provide some decent competition for him, but I know
when someone's out of my class, and I'd rather work for
the best than be second-rate on my own.'

At his age, Olivia remembered, Ross had already
established Design House and begun to lay the
foundations of his reputation and fortune. The gap
between the two men was far wider than the four years'
difference in their ages.

They came eventually to a wide doorway on the ground
floor that Patrick had avoided when they began the tour.
'Saving the best till last,' he explained, pressing down
both brass handles so that the double doors swung open
together.

She looked around. 'Have you counted them?' she
asked mildly. From floor to the small gallery that ran
round three sides of the room, the walls were lined with
bookcases. So, as far as she could see, was the gallery.
What wall was visible between the shelves had been
painted a dark green, but the paint was now in poor
condition. The books that filled the shelves were stacked
haphazardly and the random heaps on the floor indicated
where Patrick had made a forlorn effort to establish order.

'We made a rough estimate,' he said, watching her
expression. 'Between four and five thousand, we think.'

'And I thought this was a temporary job.' She

wandered over to the shelves and picked up a volume at random, then another. At last she glanced back at Patrick, who was looking slightly worried. 'I can't wait to start,' she grinned.

His relief was evident. 'Well, you'd better take the rest of today to settle in and get some ideas of the geography of the house and grounds. No one watches the clock here. Ross seems to take it for granted that everyone will work as best they can, and it's a system that works surprisingly well.' Ross, she suspected, was a fairly astute judge of character. They left the library, but she was already beginning to make plans.

'Do you want me to replace the books or are you going to redecorate?'

'Redecorate,' he said positively. 'Same green wall colour, but we might replace that dark polish on the woodwork with white enamel; it'll lighten the heavy effect of all the books without spoiling the appearance of the room.'

Clearly he had no doubts about his own work. 'Right, then—the one thing I will need is an infinite supply of boxes. Small ones—a packing case full of books is the nearest thing I know to an immovable object. I'll sort things straight into containers and label them accordingly. Is that possible?' she asked.

He bowed. 'It shall be done. Believe me, I'd find absolutely anything you wanted if it got me back to things like paint and furniture and away from those books. Tell you what, I'll bring your case up and show you your room, then we can have a cold drink outside and you can ask whatever questions occur to you.'

'Sounds fine.' She was feeling hot and travel-stained. She bent to unfasten her case and took out three large books. 'No need to take these upstairs, I'll leave them in the library.'

When she came back, she followed him up the wide staircase and along a corridor. 'Ross said to put you in here. Hope you like it.' He opened a door.

The room was delightful. Full of light and airy space, its décor suited her absolutely. And then she laughed aloud; looking almost smug in a room that at last did it justice was the little walnut desk that she had always liked and which had been hidden away in a corner of her father's shop until Ross Courtenay spotted it.

Patrick smiled. 'He told us where the desk came from.' She had already seen the tallboy in another bedroom, and the refectory table no longer overcrowded the room it now occupied. 'I hope you like it?'

'I love it, of course. You have to admit they're pretty grand quarters for staff, aren't they?'

'Don't worry, we're all very comfortably housed—what's the point of unused rooms, after all? But I must say,' he looked around, 'I've always thought this was one of the nicest bedrooms. Something about its proportions, I think. It suits you,' he added unexpectedly, and suddenly looked very young.

She laughed. 'At the moment I'm a disgrace to my surroundings. Give me an hour and I'll try to be more civilised. Will you fetch me, or do I go to the bottom of the stairs and call for help?'

'I'll knock,' he said. 'See you in an hour.'

Left to herself, she discovered the bathroom behind a disguised door and eagerly stripped off her clothes and ran the shower. She was disappointed that Ross had gone, but he had taken the trouble to meet her and there was that curious parting gesture to treasure. He might, of

course, have been being protective, sensing Theresa's
dislike, but she would have thought he was too sensitive
not to realise that it was calculated to antagonise the
woman.

She smiled as she washed away the grime of travel.
Patrick was rather sweet, the work looked as though it
might prove fascinating, and she need not fear she was
here under wholly false pretenses. She thought about the
unusual house as she rinsed her hair. Whatever state Ross
had found it in, he was clearly refurbishing it
entirely—several rooms were still empty. He hadn't
attempted to impose any sort of artificial unity on its
eccentricity; instead she had seen a highly individual
mixture of styles that was a reflection of both the house's
complexity and its owner's. And, like both, she thought,
warning herself again of her new life's more subtle
dangers, the end result had a charm that was hard to
resist.

Just as she had blown her hair dry and found a light
summer skirt to wear, there was a knock on the door.

'Ready?' asked Patrick.

'Just let me do something with my hair, and I'm with
you.' Since she planned no serious work that day, she let
the long, curling chestnut strands hang loose down her
back, merely confining their enthusiasm with tortoiseshell
combs above each ear. He watched with interest.

'Victorian?' he asked as she picked up the second
comb.

She laughed. 'You experts!' she exclaimed in teasing
exasperation. 'Anyone else notices the hair, you notice
the pins. Yes, they're Victorian.'

He was looking young again, but he grinned. 'I could
hardly fail to notice the hair, could I?' He gestured

at its abundance. 'I was just trying to impress you with my professionalism.'

'Consider me impressed. Now, what about that cold drink you mentioned?'

He led her downstairs, out through a back door she had not seen earlier and on to a terrace. It overlooked a well-kept lawn and a garden of early roses in flagrant, scented bloom.

'What wonderful flowers!' she exclaimed.

'You'd better tell Joe that. He's the gardener; he doesn't say much but he loves his roses above everything. Mrs Joe does the cooking,' he added. 'She says even less, but the food's spectacular,' he finished with enthusiasm. 'Now, what do you want to know about?'

She shrugged helplessly. 'Everything, I suppose. Particularly what the set-up is here. I thought this was Ross's private home; is he running the business from here, too?'

Patrick laughed. 'Not really. It's rather like this in London, too; we've been known to end up all over his flat, sorting out the latest problems, but in fact the main part of the business and most of the staff and work are still in London. He spends two or three days a week up there, sometimes four, and then brings odds and ends of projects down here. Miss Johnson's here most of the time at the moment.'

That made some sense, but there was one obvious puzzle. 'Where do you and Theresa fit in?'

'I'm not sure I can answer for Theresa.' He gave a schoolboy grin. 'I can guess where she'd like to be, but Ross seems happy to play a waiting game. As for me, I'm a sort of general dogsbody. Most of the people who work for Ross are specialists—like you.' It was odd to be included in such company. 'I'm the only one apart from him whose interest is all-round, and I'm staying down here to supervise the details of redecoration when he's away. I hold the other end of tape-measures and things.'

She guessed that he greatly played down his abilities. He must have talent if Ross was prepared to trust him with his own home. 'And Theresa?' she prompted.

He grinned maliciously. 'Theresa came down to look over some needlepoint on a set of chairs. Unfortunately not much needed doing, so she accepted a commission from Lady Rushton, who lives about five miles away and provides the ideal excuse for her to stay on here. The only trouble is that the work is boring her silly, and Ross won't stay still long enough for her to fix his interest. And now,' he finished with undisguised relish, 'you've arrived.'

She was about to point out tartly that there was no way she was capable of providing competition for a petite, elegant blonde with curves in all the right places, even if she wanted to, when the subject of their discussion appeared.

'Hello, you two. Idling away in the absence of our lord and master?'

Patrick didn't seem embarrassed, so Olivia saw no need to be. 'That's right,' he agreed without getting up.

Theresa perched on one of the chairs. 'This dump is really beginning to get to me,' she declared, and it dawned on Olivia just who had called the house a 'monstrosity'. 'What on earth was wrong with the London set-up? I don't believe Ross'll ever keep this place on—it's just one of his odd fancies.'

'There's nothing to stop you working from the London studio just as you always did,' Patrick pointed out. 'Ross doesn't have to check every piece of work you do.' He was obviously enjoying her irritation.

She picked up his glass. 'What are you drinking?' She took a sip and grimaced at the flavour of the soft drink. 'I'll need something stronger than that if I'm to cope with life in the country. Not to mention Ross's latest whim.' She gave Olivia a look of dislike and walked towards the house. Patrick stuck his tongue out at her back.

'You provoked her,' Olivia observed.

'True, but it was irresistible—and accurate. She could work just as well from London if she wanted to. Ross may be a perfectionist in his choice of staff, but once he trusts your judgement he doesn't look over your shoulder all the time and, whatever her personality defects, there's no doubt that madam's work is excellent.'

'Do *you* think this move is just a whim?' she asked, hoping it was not.

He shook his head. 'No. Ross may put on an act, but he doesn't go in for whims. This move's been in the air for some time. He spent large parts of last summer wandering around like Bergman, muttering, "I vant to be alone".' Olivia giggled at the vivid impression, and he went on, 'And then he inherited this,' he gestured expressively, 'and there was no stopping him. Not that he's yet shown any signs of throwing us all out and opting for a hermit's life.'

She thought of the little she knew of Ross. 'Perhaps he just likes the—*potential* for privacy?' she guessed. 'you know, lots of space and occasional islands of peace to recharge the dynamo.'

He seemed surprised, and then thoughtful. 'You may just be right,' he said slowly, looking at her assessingly.

Dinner that night was as good a meal as Patrick had predicted, but Olivia did not find it a comfortable

experience. When Theresa wasn't making her contempt
for Patrick evident, she was showing her hostility towards
Olivia or bemoaning Ross's absence. Miss Johnson said
little. Almost the only entertainment to be found in the
whole evening was to wonder just how differently Theresa
would behave when Ross returned the next day.

As it happened, she did not observe his return. She was
high on a ladder, making notes in a rapidly filling book,
when the door opened quietly and he looked up, grinned,
and left her to it.

The books were the eccentric assortment of someone
who had violent enthusiasms which never lasted long. She
suspected increasingly that among the many worthless
volumes were several that had considerable value and
historic interest, but first she had to establish a rough idea
of the subjects that were represented. She was lucky that,
on the whole, the unknown enthusiast had kept his
hobbies separate and merely filled another set of shelves
when his interest changed. At least the sorting into
separate subjects and the basic cataloguing would be
straightforward. Checking the details of editions and
evaluating them would be another problem entirely.

She emerged from her first day's work dusty and red-
eyed, glad for once of the scant protection of her glasses,
and was making for the library doors and something to
quench her thirst when the doors themselves opened in
front of her. Confused, she stopped. Behind a tray with
two glasses on it was Ross, smiling in a friendly way at
her. She blinked, took off her glasses, polished them on
the hem of her T-shirt and replaced them. He was still
there.

'Hello?' she tried.

'Hello. Patrick tells me that books are thirsty work.

You look quite thirsty.' Also grubby, sweaty and bedraggled, but at least, she decided, he was too polite to mention all that. 'I brought you a drink,' he explained.

She took the tray from him and placed it on a large copy of Webster's dictionary, the only available flat surface.

'Thanks,' she said, and coughed. 'Who's the other glass for?'

'Me. It's a reward for the effort of bringing it to you. Have you left anywhere we can sit down?'

She pushed a set of steps towards him and perched herself on the unoccupied edge of the desk before picking up her glass. 'Cheers,' she said. 'Do you wait on all your staff?'

He lifted his glass. 'Cheers. Only those who don't appear, tongues hanging out, at the conventional cocktail hour. Do you know what time it is?'

'No.' She seldom wore her watch, and the early June evenings were long.

'Seven o'clock. I'd hate you to miss dinner as well.'

She was startled. 'I didn't realise. I'd better go and change.'

'Relax.' He had somehow managed to accommodate his long frame to the steps and was looking wholly at ease. 'Have your drink first and tell me if you're enjoying yourself.'

She gestured, hands wide. 'How could I not? It's like giving a child a bucket and spade and a whole beach of untouched sand, and telling him to go and play.'

He looked round expressively. 'Mud pies might be more like it.' He frowned at her. 'Do you often wear dead spiders in your hair?'

'Frequently.' She reached up and brushed the offending web away. 'It was probably an antique, you know,' she told him. 'Most of the books in the gallery are similarly decorated. I reckon that's where the hoarding started.'

He had begun to smile as she spoke, but now he looked serious. 'Are those stairs safe? I don't know if Patrick's checked them,' he said sharply.

She took a slow sip of her drink. It was long and cold and refreshing, and somewhere in it was the kick of alcohol. She smiled at his concern. 'I must have been up both sets of stairs,' she gestured at the twin spiral staircases at either end of the gallery, 'more than a dozen times today, and moved what feels like half a ton of books. Either they're as safe as when they were built, or your woodworm are doing a lousy job.'

He lifted his own glass. 'All right. I'll get Joe to look at them some time when you're not working, but I won't try to stop you using them.'

'Good.' Her tone expressed her doubt of his ability to do so. Before he could comment, she went on, 'And you'd better choose a wet day; from all I've seen Joe's far too valuable among your roses to bring indoors just to look at some steps.' She had met him briefly that morning, and her clear admiration of his garden had won his grudging acknowledgement of her presence. She had no wish to alienate him with frivolous indoor jobs.

'I'm so glad you're settling in,' he observed, amused. 'Has Patrick filled you in on all the relevant gossip?'

'I think so,' she admitted cautiously.

'Not the orgies, satanic rites and mutilated corpses in the abandoned chapel at the back of the stables,' he explained, poker-faced, 'just the homely, vulgar things.'

She thought of Patrick's comments on Theresa and said

again, 'I think so. Is there more?'

'That depends on how much you already know. Do we keep Patrick as our go-between, or can I confide my sordid affairs directly to you?'

She suddenly saw how weary he looked. It explained the acid edge to his banter. 'Only if I can confide mine,' she told him, 'and I need time to indulge in a few. Give me six months and I'll do my best to have something worth while to offer. Besides four thousand mouldy books,' she added, putting her drink down and straightening uncertainly as he got to his feet.

He crossed the short space of polished floor between them and stood looking down at her for a moment before cupping her face in his hands, saying, 'If I weren't so tired, and you weren't so dirty, and Mrs Joe wasn't about to sound the dinner gong, I'd give you a flying start.' Then he bent his head and his lips touched hers.

It was the most delicate of kisses. Their bodies did not touch, she let her hands hang limp beside her, too absorbed in the wonder of the moment to lift them to embrace him as his mouth gently explored hers. Her lips parted on a breath and for a second she felt the kiss deepen, and then he had lifted his head and was looking down into her wide hazel eyes.

'Yes,' he said finally, his hands dropping away. 'I do have quite a talent for picking my moments, don't I? You'd better go and have a bath and drown the rest of the spiders, or Patrick will think I've been upsetting you. Go on,' he urged. 'Take the drink with you and don't trip on the stairs.'

Somehow she was out of the library and into her own room. Forget it, she told herself. He was tired and on edge and you provoked him. Don't build on it. She wouldn't. In a long race Theresa had all the advantages, and she'd be a fool not to admit it, but nor would she obey her wiser self and forget it. Some things weren't possible. She lifted the back of her hand to her mouth and felt again that butterfly touch. She stood there a moment longer, then stripped off her dirty clothes into a heap on the floor and stepped into the shower. There was still dinner, and Theresa, to face. She turned the cold tap on, full.

CHAPTER FOUR

OVER the next two weeks she saw little of Ross except with the others. They met at meals or in passing as she emerged from the library in search of boxes or fresh air, but when he was at The Folly, as even she had begun to call it, he spent most of his time in his office or working with Patrick in the farther reaches of the house. Often he was quite simply not there at all. The house had a kind of emptiness without his vibrant presence, but her own work was too absorbing for her to indulge often in the temptation to analyse her more private feelings.

Once, as they all relaxed over coffee after a meal, she had been sitting withdrawn from the general conversation, just idly watching him. He had been describing something with those expressive hands and suddenly she'd felt again their touch on her face and found herself colouring foolishly. She had taken off her glasses and pretended to clean them, looking down to hide that betraying flush. When she'd looked up again it was to find him waiting to catch her eye, a slight smile lifting one corner of his mouth. She had looked away, unable to play this game and unsure of its rules. She thought she had felt his glance rest consideringly on her more than once since then, but she had decided not to accept his challenge.

The trouble was, she thought as she brushed her hair with more than necessary vigour one evening, that she was too inexperienced. She wondered how he would react if he knew that she had never had a lover. Probably run a mile, she decided. Or opt for Theresa. Whatever her reasons, she had no intention of letting him know any such thing. His occasional flirtation and provocative teasing might be heady stuff for her untried emotions, but there was a difference between not encouraging him and trying to put him off altogether. Life, she admitted, would lose a little of its savour if he never tried to make her blush again.

Whatever the emotional undercurrents in the house, and Parick wasted few opportunites to provoke Theresa, the work went on steadily. Hers was a largely solitary operation and she ended each day dishevelled, tired and satisfied with the progress she was making. She seldom saw anything of Mrs Joe, who seemed to prefer to have her kitchen to herself, but her acquaintance with Joe himself had ripened steadily. She tended to take quiet early morning walks, as though to absorb enough fresh air to last her through the day. She and Joe often passed, exchanging only a nod or a short greeting, and now she was beginning to get a smile of sorts from the old man as well. It was progress.

With Miss Johnson she had begun to accept that her relationship would never develop beyond the polite and formal. Then, one morning, she emerged from the library to see the secretary, usually so brisk and efficient, leaning against the wall by the stairs. She opened her eyes and straightened as soon as she heard the door open, but Olivia was already hurrying towards her.

'Miss Johnson? Are you all right?'

'Perfectly, thank you, Miss Morris.' The secretary's voice was less decisive than usual.

'Are you sure?' insisted Olivia.

'Just a slight headache,' the older woman conceded

reluctantly.

Olivia looked at her closely. That pallor and frown, and the eyes that winced from the light, told a different story.

'Migraine?' she asked quietly. She had had them herself and knew that blinding pain all too well.

The secretary nodded. 'I'll be all right in a moment,' she tried to pretend.

'You won't. You should be in bed. Let me give you a hand to your room and get you some painkillers. Do you have some of your own?'

'Yes, I was going to get them. But I can't leave my work——' she began to protest.

'Nonsense. I'll plug the phone in to the library and make notes of any calls. The paperwork will just have to wait for once; you couldn't manage it anyway in your state.'

Miss Johnson gave in. 'You're very kind. Perhaps I will lie down for an hour or two.'

Slightly worried by the other woman's obvious weakness, Olivia followed her upstairs into a small bedroom she had never entered before. In the bathroom she found the pills that were needed while Miss Johnson prepared for bed. It was the clearest possible indication of her discomfort. Olivia could imagine few other circumstances in which the conventional secretary would have let herself be seen so informally. She put the pills and a glass of water by the bed and drew the curtains, shutting out the glare of sunshine. Miss Johnson's relief as she relaxed in the cool dimness was almost audible.

'I'll leave you now. Don't worry about the phone and don't get up till it's over. I'll make sure you're not disturbed.'

She shut the door quietly on the murmured, 'Thank

you,' from the bed.

The occasional ring of the telephone was not a major distraction. She took messages from most of the callers and promised that they would be contacted next day. Nothing seemed particularly urgent. She was amused by her own secretarial manner, wondering what the callers would think if they realised that the polite voice belonged to an unkempt figure sitting cross-legged on the floor surrounded by books and reference cards. Then the phone rang again.

'Mr Courtenay's office,' she said automatically. 'May I help you?'

'Promises, promises. Why do you never make me offers like that when we're together?' Ross's amused chuckle sounded in her ear. 'And since when have you taken over as my secretary?'

'I haven't.' Some instinct to protect Miss Johnson's image made her lie. 'She had to go out for a while and I said I'd answer the phone for her if it rang.'

The pause suggested scepticism, but he made no open comment. 'I see. All I was going to tell her was that I'm staying over in town this evening. I might get back early tomorrow with any luck.'

'I'll tell her.' There was a silence. She was reluctant to put the phone down and break the fragile contact. 'Have a good evening,' she said finally.

'Thanks. You should come up to town with me one day,' he said unexpectedly. 'You might be interested in the studio.' He laughed. 'And if you're very good I'll take you to the flat and show you my etchings.'

'Etchings,' she managed to say quite coolly—after all, he couldn't actually *see* her blushing, 'have always bored me. Goodbye.'

His disbelieving laugh was still in her ears as she
replaced the receiver. She felt fairly satisfied that she
hadn't entirely lost that exchange, until dinner time
arrived and she remembered that Theresa too was
spending the night in London. Uncomfortable doubts
about his evening's entertainment spoiled her appetite.

That night there was a sudden and violent
thunderstorm. It must have been the brooding humidity
that had brought on Miss Johnson's migraine, she
realised as she lay awake watching the lightning flare
outside her window. She enjoyed storms and had drawn
her curtains wide to see this one. The thunder rumbled
steadily and then the heavy drops of rain quickened into a
torrent that cooled the air. She slept deeply and woke to a
fresher day.

Outside the grass was damp under her boots and the
trees still dripped as she brushed under them, but she
almost felt like singing as she took deep breaths of the
new-washed air. Knowing, however, that her voice was
not an asset, she kept quiet as she walked on towards the
roses. Their scent would be marvellous after the rain.

Joe was there before her, his face grim. He looked up.

'Morning, miss.' There was no smile.

'Morning, Joe. What's wrong?'

He gestured. 'Can't you see it? All that rain and just
look at them.' He was disgusted.

Several of the bushes had been damaged by the storm
and one or two were knocked almost sideways.

'Take all day to put that straight, that will,' he
muttered, 'and there's some that won't ever be right.' He
looked thoroughly disheartened, and Olivia who had
never had much of a garden before she came to enjoy this
one, decided he needed encouragement.

'Then I'd better give you a hand to tie them up,' she said briskly. 'At least that'll be the quickest way to find out how bad the damage is.'

'Bad enough, I reckon.' But he had bent towards one of the bedraggled plants and was lifting it as he spoke. 'You know what to do, then, miss?' he asked.

'No, but you can show me.'

He looked doubtful, but she crouched beside him and he let her watch the deft movements of his weathered hands.

Which was why, an hour later, Ross, who had stepped round to the back of the house to stretch his legs after the long drive, found them both absorbed in restoring order to his battered rose garden. Her boots were caked with muddy soil and wisps of hair had escaped her ponytail. She reached up a hand to brush the strands back and he saw that that too was muddy, leaving a faint smudge across her cheekbone and clear skin. But her eyes were sparkling behind the big glasses, and she seemed completely caught up in her task. Joe was not far away. Ross smiled. He had never known Joe let anyone else touch his precious roses.

He walked towards them, aware of the moment when she noticed his presence and became suddenly clumsy. She looked up, sucking the finger that had found a particularly sharp thorn, and wondering why he always seemed to catch her at a disadvantage.

'Good morning,' he said mildly. 'How many jobs are you taking over?'

'Been very handy, she has,' said Joe, not looking up from his work.

'Praise indeed,' Ross acknowledged.

She was defensive. 'I always take a walk before I start

work,' she said, 'and after last night's storm——' She indicated the damage.

'It's not so bad as I feared, miss,' said Joe. 'You go on in now and I'll finish off here. I've been most grateful for your help,' he added formally, as much to Ross as to Olivia.

'That's OK. It was necessary: books can wait, the roses couldn't.' She made her own justification to her employer who, she suspected, was trying not to laugh.

He walked to the house with her. 'They can wait a bit longer. Come and have some coffee with me.'

She looked down at herself. 'I'll have to clean up first. Twenty minutes?'

'Fine.'

She had washed and changed and was passing the office on her way to join Ross when Miss Johnson called to her.

'Miss Morris?'

Olivia went in. The secretary was as neat and well ordered as ever. Yesterday's drawn figure might never have existed. 'Yes, Miss Johnson? How are you feeling?'

The stern face softened. 'Fully restored. I've just seen Mr Courtenay and I wanted to thank you for saying nothing to him about my indisposition, and to thank you very much for your kindness yesterday,' she said a little sternly.

Olivia was almost embarrassed. She sensed the older woman's dislike of an obligation. 'Don't worry about it. It's just that I've had migraine myself and I know how much I hate to be fussed, and having to give in to it,' she smiled in sympathy.

'Well, you were most helpful.' Something like friendship touched her eyes. 'I'll do the same for you if you ever need it.'

'Thanks.' Olivia left the office feeling that she understood the secretary better than she had ever expected to.

Ross was sitting on the chintz-covered window-seat in the breakfast room, and he indicated the pot of coffee on a nearby table. 'Help yourself.'

She did so, sitting down in a chair that was not too uncomfortably close. The dark blue eyes missed nothing. 'You must have left London early,' she said, to avoid the risk of silence.

'It's the least crowded time to get away,' he said lazily. 'Besides, like you, I enjoy the early mornings.' He drank the black coffee. 'Tell me how the work's going.'

She had wondered whether he needed some sort of official progress report and was glad of the chance to give him one. On this subject at least she needn't feel intimidated.

'Slowly, but well,' she told him. 'I'm afraid it'll still be at least a fortnight before everything's sorted and you can redecorate, but I think you might be pleased with some of my finds. Nothing of great value yet, but quite a lot of fascinating oddities.'

'Fits the rest of the house,' he commented, and she grinned.

'Just about. Is it all your uncle's doing or did he have some eccentric predecessor?'

'Does insanity run in my family, do you mean?'

'Well, does it?'

He chuckled. 'Let's just say that his father, my grandfather, had a very odd reputation locally. Nothing violent, you understand,' he reassured her, 'just odd.'

'That explains a lot.' Deliberately she didn't clarify whether she was talking about him or the book collection.

He looked hurt.

She told him about some of the subjects that she had found on the library shelves: early medical textbooks, studies of weaponry through the ages, a geography section that seemed fairly exclusively about South America, and various travellers' tales of distant explorations and safaris.

'Uncle Hubert,' Ross decided emphatically about the latter subject.

For a few minutes they played around with assigning subjects to either his uncle or his grandfather.

'I haven't done much with it yet,' she remembered, 'but there's a rather small and pathetic collection of early twentieth-century romances in one corner: Ouida, E.M. Hull, Elinor Glyn, that sort of thing.' She didn't tell him that she had every intention of taking one or two of the less battered copies upstairs and reading them at night in the privacy of her room, like a secret chocolate-eater indulging her vice.

'Small, pathetic and lurking in a corner describes my grandfather's second wife—not my grandmother— depressingly well, I'm afraid,' said Ross almost sadly. 'Perhaps they should be tidied up and given a place of honour.'

'You don't want to get rid of them?' She was surprised.

'Heavens, no! I told you, I like libraries to be full of books to be read, however furtively.' She adjusted her glasses busily, wondering just how much of a mind reader he was. 'Anyway,' he went on, 'after ancient anatomy, weapons of war and South American religious practices, I should think a little romantic daydreaming would be welcome. It is to most people,' he said with wistful emphasis.

She had begun to laugh at the picture he conjured up,

but his last remark irritated her. 'I wish you'd stop doing that,' she said crossly.

He made no pretence of misunderstanding her, just smiling slightly at her annoyance. 'Why?' he asked. 'You can't say I didn't warn you,' he added quite gently before she could find an adequate answer.

A sense of being hunted began to make her uneasy. She had a brief and absurd vision of her head, stuffed and mounted like one of Uncle Hubert's trophies, on his bedroom wall. She wondered if Theresa's was already there.

Fortunately for her, she later decided, the argument that she was half wanting to start with him was prevented by the entry of Patrick.

'Hello,' he greeted them both, then turned to Ross. 'Miss Johnson said you were back. I've had an idea about the turret stairs and I'll need your opinion when you've got time. By the way, did you bring Theresa back with you? Lady Rushton's flapping: she's been on the phone a couple of times and is now threatening to descend in person.'

'Olivia can offer her tea and soothe her feelings,' decided Ross, adding with a sidelong glance at her, 'She seems to be marvellously adaptable. And no, I didn't bring Theresa back. She hates early mornings.'

And that, thought Olivia, is as near as you're going to get to an answer to your questions about who he spent the evening with.

That day, for the first time, she found it hard to keep her mind on her work, and the routine of recording catalogue details seemed tedious. She was glad when she heard the hall clock strike five, and decided that for once she would break off early.

On warm afternoons, tea was served outside. She went out to the terrace but found only Patrick.

'Come and join me,' he called. 'Ross is arguing with carpenters somewhere and I can't do anything else until he's made them see sense. Fortunately.'

She had seen enough in the two weeks she had been in the house to confirm that Patrick's lazy pose was totally misleading. He could not always sustain it, and it amused her when he forgot it and was instead carried away with enthusiasm for his work. She took a cup of tea gladly.

'I've had enough for today myself,' she told him, 'so I've given up.'

'Good idea. I'm afraid you're stuck with just my company, though.'

'You mean Theresa's not back yet?' She looked sorrowful, knowing that Patrick knew exactly what Theresa thought of her.

'Oh, she's back all right,' he told her cheerfully, and did not notice the sudden, genuine disappointment that must have shown for a moment in her face. He went on, 'She came back by train and Ross picked her up at the station. I don't know what's going on between them, but she's in a filthy mood.'

Olivia did not know what was going on, either, but Theresa's temper could just as easily be the result of a lovers' quarrel as of a failure to get what she wanted. Whatever the situation, it meant that she would certainly be far from sweet company whenever she chose to join them.

That moment came sooner than either Olivia or Patrick expected or wanted. She came on to the terrace minutes after they had spoken of her, looking immaculate. She should own a country house or be lady of the manor somewhere, thought Olivia suddenly. As always, the other woman's elegant and stylish dress made her aware of her own casual working clothes. In the presence of Theresa Stanley, Olivia always felt gawky and clumsy, like a badly co-ordinated and overgrown schoolgirl. She tried to dispose her long legs in a more ladylike manner, but only managed to draw a slight frown from Theresa. She missed Patrick's appreciative glance.

'Finished already?' The voice managed to imply that Olivia was slacking badly. 'Or is the job proving more difficult than you expected?'

Whatever she answered risked sounding apologetic, so she said only, 'Would you like some tea?'

'Put plenty of sugar in it,' Patrick advised.

'And you can stop lounging around as though you owned the place,' snapped Theresa, who never bothered with subtlety or sarcasm where he was concerned.

'Why not? At least I've been getting some work done,' he pointed out in obvious reference to Lady Rushton's neglected commission.

She flushed and turned to Olivia. 'Unlike some people,' she said acidly, and Patrick was suddenly and unexpectedly angry.

'You couldn't be more wrong,' he said quietly, for once forgetting his affectations. 'She works at least as hard as anyone else in our business. And she's good. You may think Ross is impulsive, but he doesn't employ people who don't know what they're doing. Why do you think you're still with him?' he demanded, and went on before she could answer, 'He knew exactly what he was doing when he took Olivia on. She may not have the conventional experience, but since when has that worried him? She has all the knowledge, plus that intuitive

flair for excellence that no training in the world can give.
And, what's more,' he finished, 'if you weren't so
wrapped up in your own petty schemes, you'd admit it.'
He was slightly breathless and looked almost alarmed at
his own outburst, but he glared at Theresa as though
defying her to challenge him.

She was staring at him, wordless, her face flushing a
slighly mottled red. And then she put her cup down with
an ugly clatter and stalked back into the house.

Olivia was embarrassed. Touching though his
indignation was, she did now quite know how to respond
to such an obviously partisan defence.

'If she does that again, she'll break the cup,' he said
thoughtfully. 'Just like the Chelsea figure.' So that
explained Ross's comment on her first day, she realised.
He looked at her and grinned. 'I'm sorry about that,' he
went on, 'I didn't mean to explode so violently, but she
just gets on my nerves sometimes.'

'Evidently. Thanks, anyway.'

'Oh, I meant it. Every word,' he assured her. 'In fact,'
he said slowly, 'it's odd, but in some ways you remind me
of Ross.'

She was thoroughly uncomfortable. 'Now I know
you're as Irish as your name, whatever you pretend.'
Patrick came from Watford. 'If you don't want me to
blush and follow Theresa, could we please change the
subject?'

He laughed, relaxing. 'All right. My chivalry's over for
the day. You can fight any more battles yourself.'

'I think I'd rather run away,' she admitted. She stood
up and stretched. 'In fact, I intend to do exactly that. I
feel totally exhausted for some reason and I couldn't face
another confrontation, so I'm going to see if I can coax

supper on a tray out of Mrs Joe, and then I intend to disappear for the rest of the evening. Sorry if it sounds as if I'm deserting you—I am, of course, but it's not your fault.'

'Don't worry about it. Theresa will be as sweet as syrup at dinner since Ross will be there, and I'll make sure she doesn't get a chance to poison my coffee. Have an early night and I'll see you tomorrow.'

'If you survive,' she said darkly.

'Never fear.'

She didn't. There was something indestructible about Patrick's engaging good humour, and it was good to know there was someone in the house who was wholeheartedly on her side.

Mrs Joe was quite willing to send up a tray later on, so Olivia went slowly up to her room. The weariness that she had thought was simple tiredness seemed to wash over her, leaving a vague depression behind. She went up the stairs, holding the banister as though every step was an effort, although only this morning she had run lightly down them in high spirits. It was not until she had slumped into an armchair by the window that a reason for her gloom hit her: she felt lonely and, oddly enough, Patrick's support had only seemed to highlight it.

She realised as she sat there, at first too lethargic to move, that it was two months to the day since her father had died. There was no one to talk to about him or share her memories with, and even her surroundings held no part of him. Then she saw the little walnut desk, and the floodgates opened.

Long minutes later she sniffed and mopped her eyes, feeling washed out in every sense. She felt better but rather remote, as though her emotions had been numbed by her tears. It was curiously like the aftermath of 'flu, she decided, so she might as well behave like an invalid and sit and read in bed. It could be a solitary evening's indulgence and tomorrow she would feel strong enough again to cope with anything, or anyone.

Washed, her chestnut hair dried and brushed to lie loose about her shoulders, she put on a turquoise nightshirt that hung shapelessly to her knees, and got between the clean sheets of the bed. The early evening sun still lit the room and she felt sleepily comforted by her self-pampering as she picked up her book.

She must have dozed. She woke to hear someone knocking at the door and to find her book face-down on the floor and her glasses on the pillow beside her. She peered at her clock. It was after eight o'clock. The visitor must be Mrs Joe with the supper she had promised. Guiltily remembering that she had locked her door as though to bar out the rest of the world, she slipped out of bed and turned the key.

It was certainly her supper tray, but that blurred figure holding it was equally certainly not Mrs Joe.

'I earn my pocket money by working part-time as a waiter,' said Ross calmly as he walked past her and put the tray down on the bedside-table before turning round and surveying her. 'Shut that door and come back here,' he ordered, and then, seeing the doubt in her defenceless eyes, he went on more gently, 'Don't worry.' I'm not going to assault you tonight. Not even verbally,' he added as she seemed ready to brace herself for an effort. 'I just want to tuck you in.'

She walked uncertainly towards him. 'Here,' he said and perched the glasses back on her nose. 'Better?'

She nodded. He obviously recognised the vulnerability of someone trying to cope with an unfocused world. He pointed at the bed and, unresisting, she got back in and let him straighten the covers.

'Do you want to talk about what's wrong?' he asked, sitting on the bed by her knees.

'Not really. I'm not ill or anything, just being a bit daft, I suppose.' She looked down at her hands that twisted together on top of the sheet. At least Ross had met her father once. She looked back up at him, feeling childish but unable to stop herself. 'It's just that it's exactly two months since——'

She felt her eyes fill but she didn't have to finish. His arms were round her and he had cradled her head against his shoulder, his hand moving soothingly in her hair. There weren't many tears left, but it was inexpressibly comforting just to lean on him and let the grief wash through her.

She drew back at last and looked up at him with watery eyes. His hands held her shoulders for a moment longer while his dark eyes scanned her face, then he let her go and offered her a large, clean handkerchief. She emerged from its folds and replaced her glasses again, wondering if she had made a total fool of herself.

'Thanks. I don't mean to make a habit of weeping all over you.'

'If you're going to weep, it had better be on a shoulder you're used to,' he told her. 'Now, can you face something to eat or shall I dispose of it elsewhere so we don't hurt Mrs Joe's feelings?'

She was already feeling much better. 'It looks delicious,' she decided. 'I'll probably eat the lot.'

'Good. I'll leave you to it in a moment, but I took the liberty of bringing up two glasses so that you could offer me a glass of that wine.' She had not noticed the small carafe on the tray. 'Don't feel you have to, of course,' he added quickly, the hint of laughter back in his voice.

'Go on, pour it,' she told him, and accepted a glass from him. He raised his in toast to her, but said nothing.

When he had emptied his glass he stood up. 'Don't rush to get back to work tomorrow. Patrick isn't really a slave-driver, and you know I never notice anything I don't want to. Have a lie-in if you feel like it, or go and help Joe with the roses.' He smiled. 'Sleep well, anyway. Is there anything else you want?'

Totally relaxed by wine and a surfeit of emotion, she wondered for a moment what he would say if she admitted that what she wanted was to be back in his arms. Although there had been nothing sexual about that embrace, it had been like coming home. But of course she said nothing of the sort. Instead she returned his smile and said, 'Not a thing. I feel fine now, and a total fraud.'

'Nonsense.' He picked up his glass. 'Just so that no one gets upset that you've been having an orgy without them,' he said and went to the door. 'Sleep well,' he repeated and went quietly out.

She woke next morning feeling marvellous. The previous evening had a dream-like quality: even the single glass on the empty tray seemed to deny Ross's presence, and only the crumpled handkerchief she found beside her convinced her that she had not imagined everything.

She wondered for a moment if she would be embarrassed when she met Ross, but it had seemed too natural for that. She had needed comfort, he had given it. All that teasing about seduction and her confusion about his relationship with Theresa had nothing at all to do with what had happened that evening.

Despite his instructions, she was only a little later than usual getting up, but she found she was putting on her working clothes with reluctance. The storm seemed to have brought back a succession of glorious summer days and it seemed a shame to waste the unusual sunshine. She had, as yet, seen little of the countryside. She shrugged. There was a job to be done.

For once she took only a brief look outside before deciding that she needed breakfast. Patrick was the only other person at the table.

'Feeling better?' he asked.

'Infinitely. Sorry I was so moody yesterday.'

'You weren't moody at all. You did the wisest possible thing by disappearing; dinner wasn't even entertaining. Theresa was still in a temper and not hiding it well, much to Miss Johnson's disapproval, and Ross vanished before we'd finished and we saw nothing more of him. Which did no good at all to Theresa's mood, I hardly need tell you.'

'Sounds like a bad opera. I was much better off where I was.' Especially with Ross leaving the others to find out how she was and, for whatever reasons of work or boredom, not rejoining them to explain her state of mind or body. She took a second piece of toast.

She was contemplating another and collecting a cup of coffee when Patrick said, sounding amused, 'At least your appetite's not spoiled. You can't be seriously ill.'

'I'm not,' she said round the toast. 'I just had an off day. Everyone's entitled to at least one from time to time.'

'Even me?' he asked hopefully.

'Even you. But you'd better check with the boss first.'

'Check what?' Ross's voice startled her. Suddenly she

felt less hungry.

'If I could have a day off,' said Patrick, deliberately twisting her words.

'No.' Ross smiled. 'Any more problems?'

Patrick returned to apparent gloom. 'I'd hate to tell you about them.'

'Good. Is there any coffee?' He sounded very brisk and slightly pleased with himself. Olivia risked a glance at him. He was dressed even more casually than usual in a short-sleeved dark-blue skirt, open at the throat, and very faded jeans that hugged his narrow hips. He took the coffee that Patrick handed him and glanced at the two of them. 'You're very quiet. What intimate discussion did I interrupt?'

'I was just concluding that Olivia isn't very ill: she's eaten all the toast.' Patrick looked down at the half-eaten slice she had left to the side of her plate.

'I'm not ill at all,' she protested again. She pushed back her chair. 'If you're going to nag me, I'll go and talk to Joe and his roses. Their conversation is much more interesting.'

'Brain-fever. She's been working too hard,' said Patrick solemnly.

Ross surprised her. 'I agree. That's why *she*'s taking the day off.' It was the first she'd heard of it. 'Theresa's going to be busy with Lady Rushton's curtains. You,' he said firmly before Patrick could speak, 'are going to be equally busy with the tower stairs. Olivia and I,' he concluded, ''are going on a picnic.'

'Are we?' she asked weakly.

'Of course we are. Go and change out of uniform while I have a chat with Mrs Joe. I'll meet you outside the front door in half an hour.' He had gone before she could protest. She looked helplessly at Patrick, who grinned.

'Well, you heard the man: go and change.'

Defeated, and exulting in defeat, she rushed back to her room. She had no idea where he would take her, but jeans and trainers were obviously out. She surveyed her limited wardrobe.

Finally, acutely aware of time passing, she picked a pair of lime-green espadrilles and a sleeveless silk top that matched them, and offset them both with a full, swirling black cotton skirt. Her arms and legs were bare and she unbound her hair, restricting it only with the combs Patrick had noticed. The half-hour was almost up. She hurriedly added big gold hoop earring and the barest of make-up before, pausing only to pick up a black shoulder-bag, she hurried downstairs, arriving at the the bottom to find Ross waiting.

'Ready?' His smile invited her to enjoy the day. She nodded. 'Good. The basket's in the Land Rover and the sun's shining. Let's go.' He took her hand and pulled her, unresisting, with him to the door.

CHAPTER FIVE

'AM I allowed to know where we're going?' she asked as they jolted down the drive.

'I thought we'd start with a wander round Salisbury to work up an appetite, and then find somewhere secluded for lunch. Or is that too boring for you?'

It sounded like heaven. 'I think I could bear it,' she admitted, but her tone said more than her words and he smiled.

It took almost an hour to reach the old cathedral city, and they strolled round its busy streets, window-shopping in the many antique shops and small galleries. They paused before one that displayed work of local artists, and what seemed like the hundredth indifferent water colour of the cathedral spire seen from the water meadows.

'If Constable had known what he was going to start, he'd never have painted this place,' decided Ross after a judicial pause.

'Look at the other paintings.' She pointed and they both looked with awe at the garish oils of spring flowers, and then at the prices attached to them.

'We're in the wrong business,' he concluded.

'Can you paint?' she wondered.

'No, but it doesn't seem a necessary requirement, does it?' he said, wincing as he looked at the flowers again.

'I'd almost rather have the pseudo-Constables,' she agreed.

'Come on, let's go and look at the original.'

They walked down the street towards the narrow gateway leading into the Close, Ross having to drag Olivia out of the warren of an antiquarian bookshop which they passed.

'It's a wonderful place on a rainy day,' he told her. 'I'll bring you back here when the weather breaks, but at the moment you're meant to be absorbing sunshine.'

They entered the wide and grassy expanse of the Cathedral Close and craned their necks to look up at the towering spire that seemed to spin dizzyingly against the clouds. Inside, the cathedral was cool and dim and their footsteps echoed in the silence. They didn't talk much, pausing before the ancient copy of Magna Carta to read its surprisingly modern provisions and looking at the still faces of the effigies on the tombs. In the cloisters they sat for a while in the shade of the spreading cedars and then, by mutual consent, walked slowly back to the car.

Olivia wasn't quite sure when he had possessed himself of her hand, but it was comfortable to walk like that, close to him, and after last night she felt at ease and unthreatened. Deliberately or not, he seemed, for the moment, to be resisting the temptation to confuse and embarrass her.

They drove out of the city and through the lush countryside. It was all new to her and Ross seemed content to let her enjoy it, taking a winding route through little villages of brick and flint cottages, thatched roofs bright in the sunlight. She had no idea where they were going, but she realised eventually that he had a specific destination in mind.

They came to a small village, little different from the others they had passed through, and he turned the Land Rover off the main road and down the lanes until they

reached one that ended in a five-barred gateway to a field,
the church on one side of it, a farm on the other.

'I'm afraid we have to walk a little way from here,' he
told her, getting out and going round to the back to collect
the basket. She climbed down and he joined her at the
gate, holding it for her.

A narrow path led over two field to another track that
turned and passed under the railway embankment. Stiles
marked the field boundaries and she climbed easily over
them, glad of the freedom of her full skirt.

Beyond the railway there was nothing to be seen except
wide meadows, the glint of a river and a few scattered
clumps of trees. Far in the distance huddled another tiny
village.

'Down this way,' he said, turning off on to another
path and holding out his hand for hers.

'How on earth do you know about this place?' she
asked. 'Did you once live here?'

'Not really. We were brought up in London, but we
spent a few holidays in that farm opposite the church
when I was a boy.'

'I suppose that was when you were dragged over to see
Uncle Hubert?'

He smiled. 'I'd much rather have been here. I used to
fish, uselessly, for hours in the river. I learned to swim
here, too. It didn't seem to matter that the cows came
down to the same spot to drink, though mother sometimes
grumbled about the mud,' he remembered. 'Almost
there,' he said as he opened the last gate and they walked
to where the field met the river near some trees. 'Like it?'
he asked.

She looked around. They might have been alone in a
countryside that had no part in the modern world. She
could hear no sounds except for a few birds and the

distant, dull roar of the river as it met a weir further downstream.

'I love it,' she said. 'Thank you for bringing me here.'

'Always happy to please.' He spread a rug on the grass. 'I'll put the wine in the river to cool if you don't mind the primitive touch.'

'Good idea.' She lay back on the blanket, watching the clouds drift against the sky and trees above her. She could hear Ross moving around beside her, but there seemed no need to make unnecessary conversation. She closed her eyes.

She woke to a touch on her shoulder. 'Lunch time, sleepyhead.'

Ross was propped on one elbow beside her, smiling down at her with an expression she did not recognise. Confused, she sat up, straightened her glasses and tucked her long legs under the folds of her skirt.

He had laid out a simple meal of crusty bread and pâté, warm ripe tomatoes, and some soft French cheese. Glasses glinted in the sunlight and water was dripping from the winebottle. He sat up lazily.

'Help yourself,' he said, and poured the wine.

Suddenly aware of hunger, she took the glass and accepted the chunk of bread he tore off for her. 'This is wonderful,' she decided. 'I can't imagine a better spot for a picnic.'

'It's less appealing when the river floods,' he warned, 'but I'll admit it has its charm.' He seemed to be enjoying her enthusiasm. 'Val, my sister,' he explained, 'used to be convinced I'd drown myself or something. I tended to disappear all day at times, and I think she worried more than our parents did.'

It was a totally new light on someone she had always

imagined to be instinctively a city-dweller. His determination to make The Folly his home became more understandable.

'You haven't met Val yet, have you?' he went on. 'She and her husband have been away on holiday, otherwise you can be sure she'd have been over to find out all about you.'

She was not sorry to have been spared the inquisition of another Courtenay. 'Is she like you?' she wondered.

'How am I to take that? In some ways, I suppose so. She's about five years older than me, and even when our parents were alive she always tried to mother me.' He grinned. 'I'm afraid I've never been very co-operative.'

No. She could not see him letting anyone, however close, run his life for him.

'You'll meet her at the end of next week, anyway,' he said.

'Will I?'

'Yes. I forgot to tell you about her annual "do", didn't I? I think I told you she lives about ten miles from The Grange?' She nodded. He was the only one who never called it The Folly, she noticed. 'Well, she and her hsuband solve most of their entertainment problems with one large party on Midsummer's Eve. I invariably get dragged into it if I fail to flee the country in time, and I've no option at all this year since we're virtually neighbours. And,' he concluded, 'if I'm suffering, I'm damned if I'm going to let my staff off. You're all coming.'

' "Cinderella, you *shall* go to the ball," like it or not?' she asked.

'Something like that. Have some more cheese?'

'No, thanks. I couldn't eat another thing. I've never had a better picnic,' she said happily, rather spoiling the compliment by adding, 'not that I remember having been on many.'

She had kicked off her shoes and was leaning back against the smooth trunck of a beech tree. He was watching her, an indulgent smile on his face, but he frowned slightly at that.

'Don't you have any brothers or sisters?'

'No. There was always just me and Dad.' There was a trace of sadness in her voice, but she felt none of last night's aching grief. She answered his unspoken question. 'My mother died when I was three, so I don't really remember her.'

'You and your father must have been very close.' His voice was gentle.

'Very. Oh, there was a succession of motherly women who looked after me and the house when I was little, but Dad always managed to exasperate them into leaving eventually. Mostly there was just the two of us. He frequently exasperated me, too,' she grinned in affectionate memory, 'but I wasn't so easily got rid of.'

'Even when you did your library training?'

'Even then. The college wasn't far away and I was able to be at home most weekends. I always knew he couldn't really cope alone,' she explained without resentment.

He seemed curious. 'Didn't you ever rebel? Long to get away and travel, or do something different or foolish?' he asked curiously.

'Of course I did.' She sighed. 'I'm not really the village idiot I sometimes appear,' she told him. 'Besides, what am I doing now if I'm not being foolish?' she asked unwisely.

Something changed in the atmosphere between them. He did not move, but his eyes were intent on her. 'I'm not sure,' he answered slowly. 'How foolish are you willing to be?'

There didn't seem to be enough oxygen in the air and her breath quickened. She felt uncertain; exhilarated, but terrified. She made no attempt to stop him when he reached out to pull her down into his arms.

It was as though everything was happening inevitably, but in a kind of slow motion that made her acutely aware of each detail. He didn't hurry to kiss her, he held her loosely in the curve of one arm while he carefully removed the combs from her hair to give his hands the freedom to tangle in its length. Then he lifted her glasses from her and put them carefully behind a tree root. All the time she watched him gravely, her heartbeat quickening, knowing that she could and should stop him. And making no attempt to do so. Her lips were dry, but they parted as he gently traced their outline with one finger. Then he bent his head and his mouth closed over hers.

It was nothing like the kiss in the library. Her mouth opened beneath his and she felt the delicate probing of his tongue against hers. And then the pressure of his mouth hardened and became more demanding as he found the response she was helpless to deny.

Nothing in her limited experience had prepared her for the surge of feeling that swept through her at the weight of his body against hers. She reached up to hold him and tighten the embrace, revelling in the freedom to touch the thick, dark hair and feel the way it grew against his neck, and to clutch the breadth of his shoulders when the tide of passion swept her into a moment's breathless panic.

He must have sensed her sudden fear. Lifting his head, he looked down into her hazel eyes and smiled gently. His own were midnight-blue, and for once there was no teasing in his face. Hesitantly she reached up to touch him, feeling the hard strength of bone beneath the softness of skin, the slight roughness where his beard would grow. She was acutely tuned to every detail of movement and texture, and knew she would recognise him anywhere by touch alone. When she touched his mouth, his own hand came up to turn hers so that he could press a kiss into its palm.

This bore no resemblance to that courtly, half-mocking gesture he had used as a farewell on the first day she'd arrived. His tongue teased her palm's softness, and then she felt his teeth close gently on the base of her thumb so that she could not quite stifle the moan that came from her throat or stop the sudden arching of her body.

'You're very sweet,' he said. 'We should have done this the first day we met.'

'Too much snow on the ground,' she managed to remind him, only half aware of what she was saying. 'We'd have got frost-bite.'

'You seem to have lit a fire somewhere,' he chuckled, and looked down at the long, slender length of her body where it lay against his, her skirt tumbled about her knees. Beside him, she realised, she did not feel overgrown, or lanky. His long frame seemed to cradle hers as though they were a perfect match.

'We fit together well.' He echoed her thoughts.

And then his hands were moving again, tracing the neckline of her blouse while his lips made her dizzy with teasing kisses. She hardly noticed the buttons parting, but the touch of his hand against her naked flesh made her cy out briefly in shocked pleasure.

'Ssh.' He took her cry into his mouth, knowing hands finding the front fastening of her bra and parting it so that she was suddenly aware that he held her small breast in his hand, stroking and teasing its aroused crest until an unfamiliar pleasure that was almost pain seized her.

Trembling, she broke away from him but made no effort to hide herself. 'It's too much,' she managed to say in answer to the question she saw in his eyes.

'It's hardly begun,' he told her, and she shivered. He tugged her back towards him, holding her until she calmed, his hand stroking her back in a way that was both comforting and disturbing. She found herself wanting to be closer to him and, when the arm round her waist drew her hips tightly against the hard length of his, she yielded to his strength. The hand that had soothed her now closed in her chestnut hair and pulled her head back so that his mouth was hard on hers, this time in urgent demand. She responded without restraint. The knowledge that he was as aroused as she was somehow heady, and something primitive in her seemed to be urging her on. She caught briefly at sanity, wondering how he would react when he discovered her inexperience, and then she forgot it, hoping vaguely that it was a myth that men could always tell.

Then his hands had stilled on her. She looked up at him, questioning, 'What's wrong?'

He brushed the hair back from her face, teasing her swollen lips and looking down at the naked breasts that betrayed her hunger. 'Nothing's wrong,' he told her, 'except that I think I'm rushing you.'

'Wasn't that why you brought me out here?' she asked, too overwrought to find a subtler way of asking, aware also that, though she had half expected it, she did not want it to be true.

He touched her face quite gently, holding her now in

an embrace that was almost protective, and she felt the
fires begin to die in her.

'Oddly enough, no,' he said. 'Although I suppose
you've every reason not to believe me.' He laughed and
the sound was not quite steady. 'I really thought I was
offering you a day of rest and tranquillity. I should have
known better—you're far too incendiary.' He released
her and stood up, reaching a hand down to her. 'Come
on. Let's go home. We've plenty of time ahead of us,' he
added, and she knew he was not referring to the journey
back.

For a second she looked at the hand he held out to her.
All she had to do was accept it, and then tug him down to
join her. He would not stop a second time, some instinct
told her, and half of her did not want him to. But sanity
was also coming back, with thoughts of Theresa and the
uncertain future and doubts about her own feelings, so
she took his hand only to allow him to draw her to her
feet. She tidied her clothes while he bent to retrieve her
combs and glasses, handing them to her without
comment. At least *he* wasn't interested in the age of the
combs, she thought with a sudden return of humour, and
fastened them back in her tangled hair.

She left him to tidy the picnic things and went to paddle
at the river's edge where it trickled over pebbles and flat
stones. She held her shoes in one hand and stared into the
clear water, watching her flickering reflection look back at
her. In some ways she felt as fragmented as that broken
image by her brief experience of passion. She had not
known it could be like that, need overriding all
judgement, and she wanted a moment longer to collect
herself.

'What I really ought to be doing,' said Ross behind

her, a thread of rueful amusement in his voce, 'is going for a very long, cold swim. But I don't intend to, and you'd better come out of there before I push you in.'

Turning, she smiled back at him. Whatever had changed between them, the familiar Ross was still there. 'I'm coming. And I'm perfectly capable of falling in without any help from you,' she reminded him as a pebble slipped sideways under her foot and she almost lost her balance before stepping out on to the grass.

They walked slowly back to the car and he held her hand firmly for most of the way, only letting go when they negotiated stiles or gates, and he could stand back and openly admire the length of her legs as she stepped across. Aware of his eyes on her, she made no effort to stop the black shirt showing more than was necessary.

'You're asking for trouble,' he said mildly as she climbed the last gate.

'Am I?' She didn't care. Back at the house all the doubts and caution could surface again; here, just for a little longer, she would flirt as much as she liked.

'Yes.' They had reached the Land Rover and he put down the basket and pinned her against the car door, one hand on either side of her arms. 'Just try and behave like that when I haven't got a church peering over my shoulder and you'll find out,' he warned, and bent his head to kiss her once, hard, stepping back quickly before passion could flare up again.

He stared down at her then for a long moment, something very serious in his eyes, but he only said, 'We'd better go, or someone will send out a search party.'

Olivia felt slightly troubled, her daring mood broken, and got quietly into the passenger seat, not sorry for his silence as he negotiated the narrow lanes back to the main road.

He drove without urgency, although the route he took back was more direct than the one they had travelled from Salisbury. She was slightly unsure of his mood at first, but he must have sensed her uncertainty because he looked across at her, smiling gently.

'Don't worry about it,' was all he said, but she relaxed.

It was early evening by the time they reached the house, and they met Patrick as they went in.

'Have a good day?' he asked.

'Fabulous,' she admitted honestly. She wasn't sure how much he could read from her appearance, but she guessed there was no way of hidng her happiness.

'Quite tolerable,' agreed Ross beside her. 'I'll take this basket down to Mrs Joe and then I think I need a shower.' A cold one, the glint in his eyes told her as she left.

She felt her face warm. 'I'd better go and change, too,' she decided, before Patrick had a chance to comment.

She came back down to the big drawing-room a little later. Theresa, Patrick and Miss Johnson were all there, as well as Ross, and she felt absurdly shy when he smiled at her and offered her a drink. She took it, content to sit quietly, listening to the ebb and blow of conversation as Ross caught up with what had been done that day. However relaxed he might seem, she realised, his control over what was done, either for him or in his name, was absolute.

It was only after Ross had reviewed, informally but with an uncomfortable alertness to detail, what had happened in his absence, that Theresa turned lazily towards her.

'There was a phone call for you this afternoon. I was waiting for one myself, that's why I answered it.'

Olivia flickered a glance towards Miss Johnson. Both of them were well aware that nothing else would have made Theresa answer the phone. The older woman smiled fractionally and returned to the knitting that occupied her each evening.

'Yes?' Olivia asked. Theresa obviously wanted an attentive audience. 'Was it important?'

'I wouldn't know, would I?' The light blue eyes were malicious. 'Some man called Jeremy Barker wanted to speak to you.' Across the room, Olivia saw Ross hesitate as he refilled his glass. 'He sounded very keen, so I told him you'd been abducted by our respected leader, and he didn't seem to like that at all.'

It didn't sound remotely like Jeremy. She said as patiently as she could, 'That's all?'

'Not quite. He's coming down from Gloucestershire tomorrow morning and wants to drop in to see you,' she concluded.

So that was all there was to the message. 'I'll be delighted to see him,' she agreed. 'It'll be good to catch up with whatever's happened in the village while I've been away. That's the trouble with country life,' she said to Patrick who happened to be near her, 'you think you'll die of boredom for most of it, but as soon as you move away you need an update on everyone's movements.'

'Like listening to "The Archers" and missing an episode?' suggested Ross in a voice that sounded as though 'The Archers' bored him thoroughly. She looked sharply up at him. There was nothing in his face, but it was Theresa he chose to sit beside, although there was a chair free near her.

She could pin down no positive sign that gave her reason to think to herself, 'he's warning me off', but the intimacy of the afternoon might have been light years away. The usual mockery and banter went on throughout the evening meal and Patrick teased her about having an excuse for another day off tomorrow, but Ross made no comment about it. She thought at first that she would rather he had reminded her that she would be too busy catching up to indulge in a long session with old friends. By the end of the meal, however, she was determined to spend as long as she chose with Jeremy. Ross had been more attentive than usual to Theresa, evidently amused by her acid wit, and seemed almost to have forgotten their hours together earlier that day. If it had been so unimportant to him, she decided, then it was a good thing he had chosen not to make love to her fully. She could not have borne to remember that and to have it forgotten so easily by him.

She had hoped he would try to have a private word with her before she went to bed, but he had given no sign of wanting to speak to her alone. She had gone very slowly upstairs when at last she had left the drawing-room, but no one had followed her and she had discovered the dubious comfort of being 'spared the humiliation' of a rejection.

She reminded herself of all that she had feared about her feelings for Ross Courtenay. The afternoon had been a golden moment that she could neither forget nor wish undone, but it had evidently mattered far less to him and she must at least seem to treat it lightly. She got into bed wondering gloomily if experience tarnished everything. At least, she thought, Ross would be gone before Jeremy arrived. He had told her earlier that day that he had to be in London again tomorrow.

Thoughts and memories of the afternoon naturally

haunted her before she fell asleep. She had discovered at
last what passion meant. That was a lesson worth having:
she could no longer despise those who seemed utterly
subject to it. Even Theresa, she supposed, could be better
understood now. But passion seemed to have no future. It
wsa far too easily forgotten—by Ross, if not by her, she
reminded herself uncomfortably, aware of her
inexperience. If the opportunity came again, perhaps he
would want to take things further. What frightened her
was the fear that she might bc unable to resist him.

Some profound part of her longed for family, security,
permanence: the things that had never been quite certain
with her father and that she had hoped to find with
Jeremy. To delude herself into thinking that Ross wanted
to offer any of those would be the deepest kind of folly.
Wasn't that what he had called it before he kissed her?
And hadn't he already told her of his intentions?

Things began badly next day. For some reason Ross
had decided to delay his departure until the afternoon,
and he was an uncomfortably obtrusive presence.

Since she had no idea when Jeremy would arrive,
Olivia began work as usual. She had reached a section on
early herbals that looked more interesting than anything
else she had so far found. In a different mood she might
have shown them at once to Ross. Now she just made
careful notes and added them to the boxes of books set
aside for further study once the shelves were emptied.

Jeremy arrived soon after eleven. She had become
caught up in her work and did not hear the bell. The first
she was aware of anything happening was when the doors
opened and an achingly familiar voice said, 'She's in here
somewhere. Just look on top of all the ladders.'

She looked down from her high perch. Ross was staring

directly at her, as though he had known exactly where she
was from the moment he entered the room. He was
dressed entirely in black today, and his tall, lean body
looked dangerous as he lounged in the doorway. Beside
him, Jeremy's slighter figure looked frail in comparison.
He seemed ill at ease with the man near him who still had
not left the room. Slowly, feeling as though she was
abandoning a position of advantage, she climbed down to
them.

Jeremy obviously had not seen her as quickly as Ross.
Now he took in her dishevelled appearance with a slight
frown as he came forward to greet her.

'Olivia,' he said, kissing her cheek but not embracing
her. 'It's good to see you again.'

Over his shoulder she could see Ross looking as though
something amused him.

'I'm very glad to see you,' she agreed, and had the
dubious satisfaction of watching Ross straighten and
leave. 'I'm sorry I'm in such a mess, but I'll clean up in a
moment and get rid of some of the dust.'

He was looking round the room. 'It looks as though
what you need here is an army of cleaners, not an expert
on books. You're sure he's not just using you as a
skivvy?'

She glanced behind him, but the doors were firmly
shut. 'I'm positive. Put a gang of cleaners in here and
heaven knows what damage they'd do. First I sort things
out, then I make way for the brooms and dusters. I do
know my job,' she reminded him, seeing that he was still
frowning.

'Of course you do,' he agreed. 'Mr Courtenay said you
were working very hard.'

'I get time off.' She thought of yesterday. 'How long

can you stay?'

'As long as you like. I'm on my way to Southampton, but I don't have to be there till this evening, so I took the whole day off so that I could visit you.'

She was slightly surprised, but pleased that he had made such an effort.

"Come and have some coffee while I change, then we can make plans,' she suggested.

She was glad to see Miss Johnson in the drawing-room. She introduced Jeremy and left him there while she went to wash and find a neat skirt and flat shoes. When she returned, Ross had joined them. He looked at her changed appearance, but said nothing. Jeremy was talking about his work to Miss Johnson.

'What are you going to do today?' the secretary asked.

'I thought I'd show Jeremy around, then we could go somewhere for lunch and afterwards there's some shopping I have to do.'

'Don't leave on my account,' said Ross. 'I'm off in a few minutes. Where do you mean to shop?'

She had made no plans but said on impulse, 'Salisbury, I suppose.'

'And then you'll show him something of the countryside?' he suggested, and the colour flared in her cheeks.

Goaded by anger as well as embarrassment, she snapped at him. 'We'll do whatever suits us.'

He looked to where Jeremy was still talking earnestly to Miss Johnson, and then back at Olivia. He seemed to relax a little.

'I must go. Have a pleasant day.' She wondered if he had chosen the bland word consciously. He stood up, then he touched her cheek lightly. 'Sorry if I've seemed on edge. I didn't sleep well last night.'

And whether that was insult or comfort, she couldn't decide. Whatever its private message, it left her confused and uncomfortable, reminding her of everything she had been trying to lock in the back of her mind since the previous evening.

Jeremy drove carefully as they went towards Salisbury, grumbling slightly about the state of the drive. He clearly thought they could have spent the day at the house, but was also flattered that she seemed to want to be alone with him. He reassured her about the shop, which he checked daily and whose contents were soon to be collected. Ross had agreed a valuation figure with her that was more generous than she had hoped.

'And are you enjoying your work?' he asked.

'Loving it.' She could see that he would never understand, but that no longer mattered.

'What about Courtenay?'

'What do you mean?' She was defensive.

'He seemed very offhand when you were changing. Is he really any good at his job, or is it all show?'

She kept a tight rein on her temper. 'He's good,' she said firmly, and turned the subject.

Her first aim in suggesting a shopping trip had been simply to get out of the house. Salisbury had been the obvious choice as well as a chance to get back at Ross, but now she realised that there was something she should look for. If the Midsummer's Eve party was as formal as Ross had implied and Patrick had later confirmed, then she had nothing that was appropriate in her wardrobe.

She told Jeremy that she had to look in a few clothes shops, and was amused and unsurprised by his look of disappointment. 'I'll try not to take too long,' she apologised.

'All right. But can we have lunch first? I can see I'm
going to need something to give me strength.'

She supposed he could not really suggest that he left her
to do her shopping on her own, which was what she
suspected they would both have preferred. There was
something slightly comic in the situation, and she had a
lurking suspicion that Ross would have found it very
entertaining.

Over lunch, Jeremy continued to tell her about all that
was happening near her old home. Nothing much seemed
to have changed, and she was surprised at how little
nostalgia she felt. Her life seemed to have moved on a
long way in a short time.

'How's Sue?' she asked at last, thinking Jeremy was
being tactful in not mentioning her.

He looked embarrassed. 'It's not easy,' he said at last.
'I'm very fond of her, of course, but I've sometimes
wondered whether we're really suited, after all.'

'I'd have thought she was ideal for you.' She was
honestly surprised.

'Perhaps. But I still sometimes wonder . . .'
Uncharacteristically his voice trailed off. 'Will you be
coming home when this job's over?' he asked at last.

So that was why he was visiting. Either he'd heard
about the size of the sale of the shop contents, or he had
some romantic notions about first love, but he was
wondering whether they could resume their relationship.
She found herself able to view him without any irritation
or resentment, even though she suspected that he was
motivated by both reasons, and she looked almost kindly
at him.

'It's not my home any more,' she said with finality. 'I

won't be coming back.'

He seemed disappointed, but she guessed that she would see an announcement of his marriage to Sue Turner in a few months' time. She didn't expect an invitation. She pushed her chair back from the table and stood up.

'Let's go and look at clothes.'

Shopping with Jeremy was trying. He clearly expected her to know exactly what she wanted and to find it in the first major store they passed. Browsing for ideas and inspiration in a dozen small boutiques was painful and incomprehensible to him.

It quickly became a burden to Olivia. His comments were unproductive and his taste far from hers. She wondered what Ross would be like in a similar situation, and suspected that his advice might be quite constructive. He might even enjoy himself.

She was ready to give up and they were on their way back to the car when they passed a shop she had not noticed before.

'One last try?' she asked.

He groaned. 'As long as it is the last one. I don't know how you women have the stamina for this.'

He found a seat in the shop while Olivia sorted through the dresses onthe rails. There wasn't much room to see, but they seemed more individual and stylish than most of the dresses she had so far rejected, and her hopes rose.

'Can I help?'

She turned to see a girl, little older than herself, offering assistance. Aware that Jeremy was consulting his watch, she quickly outlined the situation.

'Have you anything remotely suitable?' she asked.

The girl hesitated, studying Olivia's height and colour-

ing for a long moment. 'I don't know. You may hate it,
but something came in yesterday and I think it might be
just right. Hang on, I haven't finished unpacking yet and
it's out the back.' She disappeared to return quickly with
her arms full of a material with the sheen and colour of
bronze. 'Go on,' she urged. 'Do try it, it's nothing till it's
on. I think I've got some shoes that should suit it.'

Olivia went into the cramped changing-room. The
dress might have been made for her. Strapless, it fitted
her closely until it was low on her hips, and then flared out
in a full short skirt that swirled and rustled as she moved.
When she put on the high-heeled sandals that
accompanied it she knew she had to have it. It made her
height a feature and hinted at subtleties she had never
known that her figure possessed, while the colour brought
out all the highlights of her hair. She grinned. Jeremy was
expecting her to choose something long and ruffled. She
went back into the shop to show him.

'What do you think?'

He stared as though he'd never seen her before. 'It's
very striking,' he said finally with caution. 'Are you sure
it's what you want?'

'Positive.' His comment had confirmed it.

She changed quickly and paid for the dress and shoes,
hardly wincing at the bill. Jeremy seemed glad to get
away.

They drove back to The Folly and he stopped outside
the house.

'I'd better get on,' he said. 'So I won't come in. I'm
glad you've settled in well. Look after yourself, won't
you?'

'I always do.' She brushed a kiss against his cheek,
feeling slightly remorseful about the way she had dragged

him round the shops. But at least he might feel glad to settle for Sue Turner now. 'Thank you for coming over,' she said. 'It's been a lovely day. Don't forget to give my love to Sue.' That was one message she could feel fairly sure would not be passed on.

'Of course. I'll see you again some time. Goodbye, Olivia.'

She waved as the car drove away, feeling as though she was bidding farewell to a very young part of her life, then she picked up her large carrier bag and walked into the house.

CHAPTER SIX

AT LEAST superficially, a return to her former relationship with Ross helped her through the next few days. The fact that he spent most of the time in London made it easier to cope with the situation when they did meet. Meaningless polite conversation, a little teasing and some discussion of her work seemed to be all that was necessary. It was a pity that she found it slightly depressing.

She had wondered at first whether his absence in London had anything to do with avoiding her. She should have known better: he was hardly the sort of person to be embarrassed by the aftermath of a single day's dalliance. Something had apparently gone amiss with a major project and he had to spend some time giving it his close personal attention. When even Miss Johnson was summoned up to town for a few days, she knew it was serious.

'Don't worry,' Patrick told her. 'Some sub-contractor decided to do something on his own initiative and Ross has to tear him limb from limb, get the project back to his original design and make up the lost time because there's a deadline on this one. That's all.' He grinned. 'He'll be back before the ball: Valerie's wrath is worse than the client's, and I wouldn't want to face either. Not that Ross ever seems particularly concerned by it.'

Or anything else, except possibly his work. She was coming to realise that that was probably the most important thing in his life, with women a very poor second. But she was not going to turn into another Theresa. There was no

way she would make her feelings for him so blatantly
obvious, even if she were sure what they were. Desire was
undeniable, but was that love? It would be simpler if she
could be sure the two were entirely separate; unfortunately
she feared that, for her, they were all too closely linked.

Ross was back the evening before the dance. His attempts
at salvage had clearly started well, and he was both tired and
full of high spirits: a dangerous mood that gave a sharper
edge than usual to his humour and finally sent her out of the
room, deciding that an early night was better than watching
him flirt with Theresa or mock Patrick. Not that either of
them seemed to mind. It was naïve of her to want that
gentler teasing and laughter that had marked earlier
meetings.

The next morning he came into the library just as she was
about to start work. He looked refreshed, somehow more
familiar to her, and she wanted to tell him about the books
she had found, but he stopped her.

'Tell me about Uncle Hubert's latest lunacy afterwards,'
he told her. 'First there's something else I want to talk about.
Nothing personal,' he added with a wry smile as he noted
her involuntary withdrawal.

She felt stupid, and then irritated. She should know well
enough by now that trick of his of putting people off balance
so that he could control the conversation. She sat down,
cleaning her glasses on a duster she kept in the desk so that
she didn't have to look directly at him.

'What is it?' she asked.

He gestured round the room, indicating the emptying
shelves and filling boxes and her expanding tray of filing
cards. 'You're getting on well here. Have you enjoyed it?'

'You know I have.' He didn't often ask unnecessary
questions, so what was the point of this one?

'You'll finish in another few weeks,' he reminded her. 'Have you made any plans?'

Was he trying to discover if she was going to become some sort of perpetual hanger-on? He should know her better than that. Pride made her lift her chin.

'No. But thanks to your purchase of the shop contents, plus what I'll make from the building sale,' not to mention the largely unspent salary he was paying her, 'I can afford to spend some months looking around. I'm already keeping an eye on the advertisements in the trade papers.' That was true, although she had not scanned the columns with much enthusiasm yet.

'Not getting married to Jeremy?' His voice was bland.

'Good heavens, no! If he wanted anything, it was reassurance that he'd finally picked the right girl. Which I gave him,' she added in response to his lifted eyebrow.

'I wonder if he believed you?' he said almost idly. 'Anyway, I've got another alternative for you.'

'What's that?' Her voice was carefully guarded and he smiled.

'Don't sound so suspicious. I was wondering how you would take the offer of a permanent job with Design House?'

It was the last thing she had expected. 'What?' She didn't know whether she was pleased or disappointed.

'Working for me, but on a variety of projects. Like Theresa, or Patrick, or any of the others,' he expanded. 'You can obviously cope with it, and it'll give the firm an element that's been lacking.'

'But not much missed or you'd have filled the vacancy before now,' she commented. She wasn't sure that she wanted to be 'like Theresa' in any way, especially not in relation to Ross.

He raised an eyebrow again, looking amused. 'Are you trying to talk yourself out of a job?'

'No. I'm wondering why you've created one.' If he made a crack about seducing her, she would throw the largest volume she could lift at him. And her aim was generally good.

A wry set to his mouth suggested that he too remembered that earlier comment, but his answer was serious. 'Partly because of what you're achieving here, and partly because of the present mess in London. We had to take the project virtually back to scratch,' he explained, 'and I suddenly saw how much better it would have been if I'd incorprated a library into the design instead of just book-space. Not that I want to sell books by the yard,' he must have seen her scepticism, 'but there's no doubt that they do reflect character more acutely than many other things. And there's plenty of work in renovation, too. You might quickly find yourself with too much to do, or even tempted to set up on your own.'

So he was serious. For a moment she toyed with accepting his offer and all the emotional extremes that would go with working for him. Then her sense of self-preservation stepped in.

'I don't think it's really me,' she decided.

'Give it some thought,' he coaxed. 'It could be a fascinating way of using your skills.'

The trouble was, he was right. Perhaps even more clearly than he could, she could sense some of the possibilities in the job he was offering. She shook her head. 'No. I don't think so. I'd rather take some time off and have a good look round. But I'm very grateful for the chance.'

She had never seen him angry before. He was very still and his eyes seemed inpenetrable, like flat, dark mirrors.

'It won't stay available indefinitely,' he warned.

'I didn't expect it to, I'm not putting it on some sort of list of possibilities.' She didn't want to irritate him further.

Her answer obviously didn't please him. 'I should hope not. Why won't you take it?' he insisted.

'I want to look around.' It was vague, but she was not going to tell him the truth: because I can't cope with you.

'You can look around while you're doing it. You'll have more variety and types of work than you'd ever get if you were stuck in some museum or library. Or shop,' he added deliberately, reminding her of the almost unused shelves at the back of her father's shop. It hardened her resolve. He could hurt her too easily.

'Surely that's up to me?' She had a moment's inspiration. 'I might go and work abroad for a while. There's always a demand for people with my skills in the big European museums and libraries,' she told him defiantly. She hoped it was true. From the look on his face she was beginning to think she'd have to seek employment on one of the more remote Pacific islands to get away from him. Was there a library on Samoa? she wondered wildly.

His voice was quite smooth, a polished surface covering something quite hard. 'You don't think a few years with me would give you better qualifications and experience for all this foreign travel?'

It was precisely the experience she might gain, and the inevitable heartbreak that would follow, that she was fleeing. 'No,' she said stubbornly.

'Aren't you even tempted by the thought that you might accomplish some minor revolution and make books fashionable?'

'No,' she repeated. 'And if you're so determined that this is the next element in Design House's services, then I can give you the names of three or four people who did the same course as me and would be delighted to work with the great Ross Courtenay.'

'I might just take you up on that, you stubborn idiot,' he said, all pretence at persuasion gone. 'After all, you have to be mature as well as skilful to cope with the real world.' He turned and left the library, the door shutting with a soft click behind him.

And just how mature are you being, Ross? she wondered. She wasn't quite sure why he was so annoyed. Had he taken the rejection personally, after all? He was right, of course. She was saving herself from the intolerable alternative situations of staying with him and watching him chase someone else, or having an affair and then coping with its aftermath with him still around.

I wonder what he'd do if he knew I was falling in love with him? she speculated. He might have been flattered, but he'd probably have run a mile. Attraction was one thing, love was something else. Perhaps it was a good thing he hadn't guessed that all he had had to do was kiss her and she'd probably have accepted the job and anything else he felt inclined to offer.

There was evident constraint in the atmosphere when they met at lunch. He was very attentive to Theresa's problems and sharp with Patrick, who looked puzzled. After the meal she joined Miss Johnson, expressing admiration of her knitting. She hoped that the slight friendship she and the secretary had established might afford her some protection. There was certainly something like sympathy in the other woman's eyes as she held up the dark red sleeve she was working on.

'I enjoy knitting,' she said, 'and I'm fortunate in having a large supply of nieces and nephews to give the results to.'

'Are you going to tonight's dance?' asked Olivia. If she didn't think it might provoke an explosion, she would have stayed at home herself. She wasn't sure she wanted to meet Ross's sister.

Miss Johnson shook her head. 'No. One of the privileges of my age is that there are some things even Mr Courtenay can't persuade me to do.' For a moment Olivia wished she were fifty. 'Have you a nice dress?' the secretary asked.

Nice? She wasn't sure. 'Well, I like it.' She grinned. 'I only bought it last week and I'm just realising why women used to have maids. I'm going to have to be a contortionist to do it up.' In the shop, the assistant had helped with the critical bit of the zip, and the last hook and eye.

'I'll do it for you. I always like to see what people wear even if I don't want a ballgown myself. I'll come and knock on your door at about half-past eight, if you like.'

She was surprised and pleased. 'That would be marvellous. And you can tell me if you think I'm being outrageous and would be better off dragging out a safe long black skirt.'

'I doubt it, but I'll certainly come along. And now,' she put the knitting back in its bag, 'I must get back to work. I'll see you later.'

Ross had been too far away to hear their conversation, but he was watching her with a kind of glinting curiosity that made Olivia decide she would be better off out of his way. She put down her cup and left the room, half wishing she could lock herself into the library for the afternoon.

Whatever her fears, she was undisturbed, although she did little useful work. She saw nothing of anyone else when she gave up for the day. Theresa at least was probably giving her full attention to her preparations for the evening. Olivia hoped the result would be so effective that Ross wouldn't

even notice her. Then she grinned. If that happened, she'd
be so jealous she'd probably try to sabotage Theresa's hair-
do.

Amusing herself with images of the two of them fighting
tooth and nail over a totally indifferent Ross, she began her
own preparations. She told herself that she could cope
perfectly well if she looked at it as some kind of play in which
she had only a minor part. She might have to arrive with
Ross, but surely she could rely on Patrick to be her real
escort?

She was wearing a loose robe and drying her hair when
someone knocked at the door. She looked at the clock. Miss
Johnson was early. But it was the cook who stood outside.
She held a small gift-wrapped parcel in one hand.

'I was asked to give you this, miss,' she said, and walked
away before Olivia could ask any questions. She stared down
at the little box. It was very light.

Back in the room she opened the parcel almost
reluctantly. Inside was a clear cellophane box holding a
single orchid. There was a note attached and she opened it,
knowing who it was from even before she saw the decisive
handwriting.

'Dear Cinderella,' she read. 'Can we call a truce? I'm
sorry I was in such a foul mood this morning, even if I still
think you're wrong. Will you dance with me if I promise to
behave? Ross.'

Not Prince Charming. This man was altogether more
dangerous. If she had any sense at all she would leave the
flower in its box on the dressing-table. But she knew she
would wear it. She put the note safely away in a drawer of
personal valuables. So what part did she have to play now?
Suddenly she no longer wanted to be a spectator, and she
was glad she had bought the extravagant dress.

She had just finished the awkward task of putting in her contact lenses when Miss Johnson arrived.

'I didn't know you wore those,' she commented, seeing the case.

'I don't often. I've never built up a tolerance of more than a few hours, but even if I have to remove them before the evening's over and spend the rest of the night peering sightlessly at my partner, I don't think I want to wear glasses with that dress.'

Miss Johnson looked to where it was spread out on the bed. 'Understandable,' she said drily. 'They might go with the long black skirt, but not with bronze taffeta. What goes under it?' she added, and then looked embarrassed at her own question.

Olivia grimaced. 'Me, and not much else,' she admitted. There was no way of wearing a bra or slip with that dress, and she could only be glad for once that her figure needed no support. There were occasional advantages to being underdeveloped.

'Well,' said the secretary briskly, 'let's see it on.' Olivia slithered rather self-consciously into the dress and turned her back, lifting her hair so that the other woman could pull up the zip and complete the fastening. 'Turn round.'

She turned, and the skirt rustled and swirled. 'What do you think?' she asked, feeling slightly anxious.

'It's not what I was brought up to call a ballgown,' said Miss Johnson judicially, 'but you've certainly got the figure to carry it. You look lovely.'

'Thank you.' She was touched by that unexpected approval.

'What are you going to do with your hair?'

Olivia lifted and twisted it, revealing the long line of her neck. 'I thought I'd put it up.' She was hoping for a touch of the sophistication that Theresa knew so well how to achieve.

'If you'll take my advice, you'll wear it loose,' Miss Johnson said finally. 'Just draw it back at the sides with those pretty combs you sometimes wear.'

'Won't it look too casual?'

'With that dress?' She laughed. 'I think one or two people are going to be quite taken aback tonight.' She noticed the flowers on the dressing-table. 'What a lovely orchid! And it'll be just right with the dress.' She frowned. 'You don't want to spoil the line, though. How will you wear it?'

She had already given that some thought. She held up a short length of bronze velvet ribbon. 'On my wrist, if you'll help me?'

'Perfect. Do you want it sewn on?'

That had been her first intention. Now she shook her head. There would be an uncomfortable symbolism about being so firmly bound to Ross's gift. 'No, I'll put a hook and eye on if you'll help me get the length right.'

It took no more than a few minutes, and a couple of stitches held the flower itself in place on the ribbon. She slipped if off. 'I'll put it on again when I've done my face.'

'You wouldn't want to damage it,' Miss Johnson agreed. 'I'll leave you now. I hope you have a splendid evening, and thank you for letting me see the dress.'

'Thank you for all your help,' said Olivia with real gratitude. 'Goodnight.'

She went back to the mirror and began the tricky business of putting on her make-up without disturbing the lenses that she was unused to. Tonight she wanted to be more dramatic than usual. Finally she was satisfied. She slipped on a plain gold necklace and earrings. She wanted no fussy details detracting from the dress, the flower was its one exotic touch.

She put on her shoes and stepped back to look in the full-length mirror. She hardly recognised herself, and lifted one hand cautiously to touch the hair that tumbled about her shoulders. Her image lifted its graceful hand with the flower emphasising the slenderness of the wrist and pushed back the chestnut curls. So it really was her. She wondered uncertainly if she could live up to the reflection that was regarding her so seriously. Then they grinned at each other. Nothing was going to make her wear the long black skirt, and at least her clothes wouldn't turn to rags at midnight.

She closed the bedroom door firmly behind her and walked slowly down the wide staircase.

Patrick was standing at the bottom. He must have heard her approach because he turned round as though to greet her casually. Then he simply stared. It was, she realised, a very satisfying reaction.

'My God,' he said at last, 'you look fantastic.'

She bobbed an absurd curtsey. 'Thank you kindly, sir,' she said, smiling. 'You don't look bad yourself.'

In his dark evening dress he looked both attractive and rather young. He had the sort of appealing looks that would get attention from women of all ages.

'Am I the last down?' she asked.

'Heaven's no! Theresa would never let that happen, although I suspect you've already stolen her thunder. She's still upstairs, but she won't make her entrance until Ross gets back.'

'Gets back?'

'From getting out his respectable car. Neither of our cars takes more than two, and even he's not going to go to a ball in a Land Rover. If we have to toss for partners,' he went on, 'I'm going to use my favourite double-headed coin.'

She laughed. 'Thanks. But I'd have thought the distribution would be obvious.' It certainly was to her, and she wondered for the first time if he had sent a flower to Theresa as well.

'Not to me, it isn't, but I've a depressing feeling I'm going to draw the short straw,' Patrick murmured.

Before she could comment, Ross himself came in through the front door. If Patrick was attractive in evening dress, he was stunning. The dark clothes and severe tailoring only emphasised his dramatic looks and height, and there was something very masculine about his easy grace.

His eyes narrowed as he saw her, flickering over her dress and settling briefly on her wrist. He smiled.

'Good evening, Cinderella. I've just brought the pumpkin round.' He crooked his arm for her and she automatically tucked her hand into it, aware again of how well their heights matched, even with her high heels.

'I told you so,' grumbled Patrick. 'You do realise you've just ruined my evening, don't you?' he said to Ross, who grinned.

'The rewards of power,' he told him, then asked, 'Is Theresa ready?'

'Coming,' called a voice from above, and she ran lightly downstairs as they all turned to watch.

'Told you so,' whispered Patrick to Olivia, and she thought she saw Ross's lips twitch.

Theresa was in light blue that frothed and billowed in delicate profusion, hinting at the figure beneath without revealing more than the swell of her breasts. She wore no flowers. She looked enchantingly pretty, however, and very feminine. Olivia expected Ross to release her arm at once to greet her, but he only said, 'Very nice, Theresa,' before turning to Patrick. 'I'll take Olivia with me and you bring

Theresa. We'll meet up at Val's. You know the way?'

Patrick nodded. He was watching Theresa, who was just beginning to realise what was happening and whose expectant expression was changing rapidly. 'If I survive,' he muttered.

When Ross got her out of the house and into a low-slung black sports car before the first protest came, Olivia didn't know whether to sigh with relief or giggle. She looked at Ross who was watching her, a challenging gleam in his eye.

'Nicely managed,' she said, adding, 'I always forget—is it the rat or the lizard who drives the pumpkin?'

He chuckled. 'Thanks. Whichever you prefer, of course. Just cross your fingers that it doesn't collapse at the first pothole. Then it will have to be the Land Rover, after all.'

With him beside her she wouldn't have minded if it had been a combine harvester. The short journey through the dark lanes had an excitement that had not been present during their last drive together, and it had nothing to do with the powerful car.

'Thank you for the flower,' she said, breaking the silence that had fallen between them.

'Thank you for wearing it. You realise it means you'll have to dance with me?'

'I decided it was worth the sacrifice.' Keep it light, she told herself, and you just might survive. She wasn't convinced that she wanted to.

They drew up at last in front of a sprawling manor house whose open windows and door spilled light and music onto the gravel. There were coloured lights in the trees and a marquee on the lawn.

'She's done herself proud this year,' he commented. 'All we have to do is find her.'

Olivia was very uncertain how she felt about this meeting,

but with Ross as her partner she began to think she could face anything.

They waited a few minutes until the other car drew up, and went over to greet its occupants. Ross grinned at Patrick's hunted expression and Olivia took in Theresa's look of frustration with her own private amusement. She might have to pay for it later, but tonight she could be the possessive one. She reached out for Ross's arm and found her hand taken warmly in his.

'Ready?' he asked, as though sensing her nervousness.

'Ready,' she agreed.

The hall and the rooms on either side of it were already full of people, but Ross's height gave him an advantage. He looked round for a moment and then said, 'Over there.'

In the crowd Theresa had to hold on to Patrick's hand to stop herself being separated from the others and, noticing it, Olivia wondered which of them was enjoying it least. Then she stopped noticing them altogether.

Ross's sister had his dark hair and something of his height, but her eyes were brown and the bone-structure that was so attractive on him was slightly too forceful for feminine beauty. But she certainly had presence. Val Standish would command attention anywhere.

'Ross!' She embraced her brother with evident affection, then she turned to Olivia and her eyes widened. 'Who's this?' she demanded.

'Olivia Morris. I told you about her,' he said simply, his hand still possessing hers.

'I think you probably missed out all the important details,' said Val slowly, 'which is very unlike you.' She smiled at Olivia, who suddenly realised that this striking woman had charm and humour as well as authority. She was not so unlike her brother, after all. 'I'm delighted to meet you,' she was saying. 'What I'd really like is a long talk, but this doesn't seem an opportune moment.'

'It certainly isn't,' her brother interrupted. 'I'm going to take her away and dance with her, and you needn't expect to see her again this evening.'

'I won't. But you can expect a visit some time in the next few days.'

'We'll fly the country. Look, here comes Patrick and Theresa. Do be energetic and a good hostess and separate them; Patrick deserves to enjoy himself.'

'And Theresa?'

He shrugged. 'I'll leave that to you.' He kissed his sister's cheek briefly. 'See you. Come on, Olivia.'

She laughed. 'Yes, O master, but if I fall over in these shoes, it's your fault.'

Val's amused and speculative gaze followed them as they made their way to the source of the music.

'Where's Val's husband?' asked Olivia as they strolled across the lawn.

'Charles? Hiding in the billiard-room, I expect. He hates these occasions but agrees it's best to get it all over at once. Especially since he need only emerge from time to time to be civil to a few neighbours. You'd like him,' he added irrelevantly, 'and oddly enough Val does what he wants most of the time,' he told her, as though he could see that might be hard to believe. 'And now,' he said as they reached the dance-floor laid out on the grass, 'let's forget everyone else for a while.'

He took her in his arms and it didn't seem to matter that they were surrounded by thirty other couples. They were enclosed in a private world of his making, where slow music let her be close to him without doubts or resistance. His hands held her firmly, and she was aware of the movement of his body against hers as well as of the texture of his jacket beneath her fingertips, but neither of them sought to tighten the embrace. Unspoken was the knowledge that they had all evening before them and no decisions had yet been made.

Eventually the music quickened and people around them began moving to the livelier rhythm. She thought she felt his lips brush her hair, and then he was stepping lightly away from her.

'Shall we take a walk?' he suggested.

They wandered through the moonlit garden and under trees where coloured lights flickered in the faint breeze. She stumbled once when her heel caught in a soft piece of ground. She heard his soft chuckle as he steadied her, but he moved over to a flagged pathway where her footing was more secure.

Occasionally people called Ross's name and he returned a greeting, but it must have been obvious that they were too absorbed in each other to welcome company. His arm was round her shoulders and she leaned against him in contentment.

'We're not being very sociable, are we?' she commented, adding, without conviction, 'Oughtn't we to mingle with the others?'

'I spend most of my time surrounded by people. I've done my duty as far as Val is concerned by turning up, now I want to enjoy a peaceful interlude. Preferably with you.' He looked sideways at her, smiling.

'Good,' she said quietly, and wondered just how big a step she had taken to commitment.

They came eventually to a small rose border. 'Not as good as Joe's,' she commented.

'Her gardener lacks your support.'

'Her roses lack Joe's,' she said, her eyes critical.

Among the people in the distance she thought she saw Theresa laughing animatedly up at someone she didn't recognise. Either Val had done some successful manoeuvring, or Theresa had decided to make the best of things. Ross saw her too, but all he said was, 'Patrick should manage to enjoy himself now.'

'I expect he will. He's so likeable that he's welcome anywhere.'

Ross looked down at her. 'He's also more than half in love with you .'

'With me? That's silly, he's just a friend.' She didn't believe him, but he was serious.

'He'll grow out of it, eventually, but I've seen the way he looks at you.'

She was distressed. 'I didn't know. I just thought he was being kind—I didn't mean to encourage him.'

'I know.' Ross did not seem very concerned. 'It was probably inevitable, considering the war that's been going on between him and Theresa ever since they met. As soon as you became her victim he was bound to become your champion.'

'I didn't notice you springing much to my defence,' she reminded him.

'It didn't seem necessary. I thought you could probably cope perfectly well on your own and, besides, there was always Patrick.' He did not need to point out that any intervention by him would only have made things worse. 'I heard his brilliant defence of you the other week,' he added.

She remembered that ugly scene on the terrace. 'You did? How?'

'I was coming out for some tea. And then I changed my mind.'

'And stayed to listen?'

'Naturally. I agreed with everything he said, you know.' He lifted his hand briefly from her shoulder to touch her neck. 'You're very good at your work.'

She laughed, shaken. The combination of such a tribute with the unspoken current of physical desire that was running fast between them was too heady to cope with. She moved away from the shelter of his arm to a wooden bench and sat down. He joined her, not touching her, giving her the breathing space she needed. To keep the conversation away from what was happening between them she spoke again of Patrick.

'He's very talented, isn't he?'

'Yes.' He accepted her lead. 'He only needs more confidence. If I can't make him branch out alone soon, I think I'll have to take him into full partnership.''

'He'd love it.'

'It would mean I wouldn't have to be so involved in every project. I could be selfish and just indulge in those I really wanted to do.'

'Why did you choose the design business?' she asked.

'It chose me. Originally I studied architecture, but it was always the interiors that intrigued me: the way people from cave painters onwards have softened and highlighted the shapes around them with things like paint and fabric and furniture has always fascinated me. It's so revealing. And I hate it when some beautiful room is ruined just because someone can't see its potential.'

'So everyone has to follow the taste of the great Ross Courtenay?' she asked.

'Not at all. If they've none of their own, I'll create something a damn sight better then they ever will—and they'll never see the difference and never add the personal touches that makes a place really individual,' he added with momentary exasperation. 'But if they do have a vague idea of what they want, and most people do, I can show them how to achieve it and that's very satisfying.'

It was the first time she had heard him reveal something of what motivated him, and she was intrigued. 'What happens to people who can't afford you, I wonder?'

She saw his grin in the dim light. 'It's amazing how many people have managed perfectly well without ever having even heard of me.'

'But once they've discovered you——?'

'Ah. That's different. Once they've tried me, they're spoiled for anyone else.' A wicked glint in his eyes warned her that the conversation had moved away from the professional to something far more personal. The trouble was, she feared that he was right. That was why she had been fighting him. But tonight, she knew, the fight would be over. She was near to surrendering, but did not know how to tell him.

It was he who found the words. He had been watching her profile, reading her anxieties and hesitations; now he reached out to lift back a tendril of hair that had fallen over her shoulder and she knew he felt her shiver.

'Shall we go home?' he asked, simply.

They would leave the noise and the coloured lights behind them, and there would be no one awake in the big house.

'Yes,' she said, not looking at him, knowing what would happen and glad of it.

CHAPTER SEVEN

HE DROVE slowly back to the house, the black car slipping away unnoticed from the revelry. Beside him Olivia was uncomfortably nervous. If only he could just have taken her in his arms and swept her up into the passion she remembered so vividly, she wouldn't have had time to think about what she was doing. This journey, and the half-informed knowledge of what awaited her at the end of it, revived all her uncertainties. She was intending to do something she had told herself would be madness ever since she had first suspected what she might feel for this man. And she could not fool herself into believing she was simply carried away by his expertise. If this was seduction, it was far more subtle and dangerous that she had ever expected. He had seemed to allow her every chance to refuse him, and now her own weakness was proving his strength.

The journey was almost too short. The car drew up and he got out, coming round to open her door as she slowly undid her seat-belt. He did not touch her as they walked up the steps to the front door and he unlocked it, closing it quietly behind them. In the dimness of the hallway, a clock was striking midnight.

'Pumpkin time,' he said softly beside her, and she stifled a nervous giggle. He was watching her closely. 'Come on.' He took her hand and they walked together up the wide staircase. She shivered slightly as they stopped outside her bedroom door, and he turned so that he could look into her eyes.

'Cold feet?' he asked, his voice understanding all her fears and accepting them.

'A little,' she admitted. 'But . . .' She didn't know how to explain herself, and it seemed she didn't need to. He touched his finger lightly to her lips.

'Don't worry about it. Go and take out those lenses while I find us something to drink. At least we can raise a toast to each other.' He dropped a quick kiss on her lips and stepped back. 'Go on.' He opened her door and urged her in.

The lenses were beginning to hurt. Carefully she took them out and then cleaned the make-up from her face. She thought about changing out of the dress, but the fastening was stiff and hard to reach. She had a momentary vision of sleeping in it and then slipping along early to ask Miss Johnson for help. No. She would rather manage by herself, even if it meant damaging the lovely fabric.

Was he expecting her to go along to his room? Or would he come here? She wasn't sure if he was waiting for her there, or what she ought to do. Books always hurried over the awkward little decisions that were so hard to make. Hesitantly, she picked up her glasses and walked barefoot to the door. Before she reached it, however, he had knocked and opened it. His white shirt was open at the neck and he had removed his jacket.

'Come along,' he said. 'You never did get any champagne and you certainly deserve at least one drink.'

'Do I? Why?'

'For making Patrick speechless? For wearing my flower?' It was still on her wrist and he smiled down at her. 'For courage?' He opened the door to his room which was lit by a single lamp. There was nothing threatening here: a simple harmony of blues and browns, a made-up bed, a bottle and two glasses on a table. He poured the sparkling wine. 'To us?' he suggested.

In silence, watching him gravely, she lifted her drink, accepting his toast. She had only taken a sip or two when he took the glass from her.

'Let's see if we can do anything about the cold feet,' he said, half teasing, and drew her into his arms.

It was where she had ached to be, even when she had most feared it, and her doubts melted at the touch of his mouth on hers. Delicately, his lips teased hers, and then he kissed her eyes and brow, drifting towards the sensitive spot below her ear as her breath quickened in pleasure. She lifted her arms round his neck, feeling the soft cotton of his shirt and aware of the muscles of his wide shoulders. His hands travelled over the bare skin of her back.

He lifted his head, holding her close to him. 'This is a wonderful dress,' he said, quietly.

'You like it?' It seemed to her an odd moment for such a comment.

'I love it. It's as stylish and individual as everything else about you,' his voice held sudden laughter, 'and I've spent a large part of this evening wondering what keeps it up and how I can get it off,' he admitted cheerfully.

Her own chuckle answered his, although the movement of his hand in her hair and the soft kisses that punctuated his words were having a devastating effect on her.

'I know what keeps it up,' she managed to tell him, 'but I had to get your secretary to fasten it, so I've no idea about your other problem.'

This time he laughed aloud, sweeping her off her feet in a hug of sheer exuberance. 'You're wonderful, did you know that?' He put her down. 'Come here.' He drew her to him with one arm around her waist so that her head rested against his shoulder. 'Now, let's see.' His free hand explored the dress's fastenings. 'Yes, I think I've got it.' He lifted both hands to his task, murmuring. 'A man could happily drown in your hair,' as he lifted its strands aside.

She felt the zip move downwards, glad that he could not see the colour in her cheeks. She turned her mouth to his neck, feeling the pulse that beat quickly under her lips, and knew that he was less controlled than he seemed. The glittering fabric slipped from her and fell in a pool at her feet as he lifted his hands. He stepped back, surveying her body, naked now except for her flimsy briefs and the band on her wrist.

'You're perfect,' he said, and then he lifted her on to the bed. Never before had she known what it was to feel light in a man's arms. She lay there, reaching out to draw him down, but he resisted. 'In a minute. I'm beginning to feel overdressed.'

He stepped away and she heard the sounds of his clothes being dropped carelessly to the floor. She was glad for once of her short sight and the glasses abandoned on the table. Except for glimpses in films, she had never seen a naked man, and the blurred quality of the world was a temporary relief. Then he was beside her on the bed, and the nearness and warmth of his body against hers drove out her fears. She gasped when he drew her to him, but the force of her own desires arched her against him in ardent response. After that picnic she had wondered, half-ashamed, how his skin would feel under her hands. Now that she knew, the excitement was beyond her imaginings. Her breasts against his chest made her aware of the differences in textures, her softness vulnerable to his hardness and the rougher brush of hair against her skin.

He lifted away from her slightly so that his hand could rediscover her breasts, and then his lips were where his hands had been and her fingers had tightened in his hair at the shock of pleasure. He lay there for a heartbeat, his head between her breasts, his hand caressing the flat plane of her stomach above the briefs she still wore. And then he lifted his head and looked at her.

'Has anyone done this to you before?' he asked quietly.

Hardly knowing what she was saying, longing only for his hands and mouth to continue their exciting explorations, she admitted, 'No,' and moved against him.

He reached up to cup her face, turning her so that she had to meet his gaze. At this distance, even she could see that he was serious.

'Why not?'

Unexpectedly, she wanted to giggle. How did you explain your virginity away when all you were hoping was that you were about to lose it? But he still awaited an answer.

'I don't know,' she admitted. 'Jeremy never insisted and everyone assumed he and I would marry, so no one else showed much interest. I think I always assumed, if I thought about it at all, that I wasn't a very passionate person.' How wrong could one be? 'Anyway,' she went on, gratified by his shaken laugh, 'life in a small village tends to be awfully public.' She remembered her irritation when neighbours or passing cars had interrupted their embraces, and Jeremy's embarrassment. 'Does it matter?' she asked, suddenly uncertain.

'It makes a difference,' he said, still holding her, 'but I'll try to overcome my prejudices. Just this once,' he added.

'That's all it takes,' she reminded him, and felt again the movement of his laughter against her. It had never occurred to her that passion could also be fun, and she was finding it a heady mixture.

But he was serious again for a moment. 'The trouble is,'

he said slowly, 'that I have to hurt you. And I don't want to. All I want to do is to please you.' He was stroking the hair back from her face, and neither hand nor voice were quite steady.

She tightened her own hands on him. 'It has to be some time, and someone,' she told him. 'And I want it to be you. Now.'

Despite her inexperience, she recognised the responsive tremor that ran through him at her words. Then he kissed her lightly. 'So be it. Come here and let's see what we can do together.' He drew her closer, pausing to release the band from her wrist, dropping a kiss in its place, before returning to his exploration of her body.

At what point she lost her last garment to the intimate caresses of his hands, she never knew. Dizzy with desire, she melted beneath his touch and learned at the same time that her hands on him could make him shudder with pleasure. He teased and soothed and aroused her with an understanding of her body that half shocked her with things she had never known about herself, until she was almost begging for his possession.

'Please,' she whispered, moving uneasily beneath his hands.

The midnight eyes held hers, and then his lips on hers demanded all that she had to give as he moved between her legs, taking her brief cry of shocked pain into his mouth and soothing her before he moved again. Gently at first, and then with a rising urgency that caught her in its spiral, he took over her body so that she was helpless except to be swept with him into an unknown world of feeling that half frightened and then utterly overwhelmed her. She cried out his name, 'Ross!' as she lost control.

His own cry followed hers, but she hardly heard it. She lay

in rich darkness, aware only of a physical and emotional
satisfaction she had never imagined. She did not even know
there were tears on her cheeks until she felt gentle fingers
brush them away. She lifted eyelids that felt unnaturally
heavy. He was watching her with tender concern, and
something else she was too tired to decipher.

'Ross?' she asked sleepily.

'Yes, love. Are you all right?'

It was an effort even to laugh. She smiled instead. 'I don't
know. I've never felt like this before. I think so,' she answered
vaguely.

He chuckled. 'Good. Go to sleep now, darling. We'll talk
in the morning.'

She couldn't imagine what there was to talk about, but
sleep was washing over her in waves and she could not resist it
much longer. She struggled to sit up.

He pulled her back. 'Where are you going?'

'To bed.'

'You're in bed,' he reminded her, amused. 'And if you
think you're sleeping anywhere else tonight, hard luck.' He
turned her so that her back was tucked against the front of his
body, curving himself protectively round her. 'I told you we
fitted together, didn't I?' he said as she snuggled closer to the
form that had become so intimately familiar. She stifled a
yawn and he laughed, kissing her shoulder lightly. 'Go to
sleep,' he ordered again, and she hardly heard him.

She woke to find the room flooded with early morning light.
There was no moment of unreality or uncertainty: memory
and sensation were with her before her blurred vision had
absorbed the unfamiliar patterns around her and the warm
shape beside her. She turned on the wide bed, and groaned.

'What's wrong?' He chuckled, obviously reading her

expression accurately.

She lay back against the pillows, looking up at the figure propped on one elbow beside her. 'I'm so stiff, I can hardly move,' she said accusingly.

'Poor love.' He bent and kissed her gently, tasting the slightly swollen lips and then looking down at her naked body with pleasure as well as sympathy. 'What you need is a day in bed.'

'How do you think I got into this state?' she demanded, responding despite her aches to the hand that was gently tracing her body. He laughed and reluctantly let her go.

'Alone, I meant. First a long bath, then you can catch up on all that lost sleep. How does that sound?'

It sounded wonderful. But then all the complications of reality returned to her, and she sat up stiffly. 'I can't. It'll be too obvious . . .'

'And you don't want people to know? They might guess when they see you, I suspect.' He frowned briefly. 'Why don't you come up to London with me instead, then? I ought to go there today or tomorrow, and you could stay at the flat. Then you needn't see anyone.'

'They'll still guess.' The thought of Patrick's disappointment and Theresa's venom seemed suddenly more powerful than the loving intimacies of the night.

'Not necessarily. You must have some things you need to check out at the British Library or somewhere?'

'Yes, but . . .'

'And they're going to have to know some time.' He tilted her head so that she had to meet his eyes. 'It might be best for me to leave you alone for a day or two,' he admitted gently, aware of her discomfort, 'but last night was a beginning, not an end,' he told her firmly.

Of what? It was the important question that she dared not

ask because she already knew the answer. He would be a caring and tender lover, and even when it was all over he would try not to hurt her, but she already knew that it would never be all over for her.

'I'll stay here,' she decided. It was both pleasure and pain to be close to him, and she did not feel emotionally or physically able to cope with either.

He was frowning again, trying to read what lay behind her reluctance, but he did not press her. 'Whatever suits you. Shall I put London off?'

'No. I'll see you when you get back. Give a girl a chance to recover?' she pleaded, only half joking.

He grinned down at her. 'You think I'd be better off out of temptation's way? You might be right.' He picked up his watch from the beside-table and grimaced. 'If you're intent on preserving your reputation, you'd better go soon. But first . . .' He leaned over her, watching her eyes for a moment before letting his mouth search hers in a long and tender kiss in which the embers of passion flickered. He drew away. 'That's just in case I forgot to say "thank you",' he told her. 'And now, if you don't want me to forget all my resolutions,' he glanced down at his quickening body, 'you'd better run.'

'Hobble, you mean.' Reluctantly she eased herself from the shelter of his arms, retrieving her few scattered belongings from the floor and her glasses from the table.

He watched her, a smile playing round his mouth, as she stood there holding the crumpled dress and wearing only her glasses. 'There's a bathrobe behind that door,' he offered.

'Thanks, I'd hate to shock the rest of the household.'

'And I'd hate them to see you like that,' he admitted with unexpected possessiveness. While she shrugged into his ample robe, he opened the door. 'Coast's clear.' She would have passed him, but he stopped her. 'I'll probably be gone when you next surface. Don't work too hard. Barricade the library door and go to sleep or something, and make sure you dream of me.'

Waking or sleeping, she knew she would. She reached up to kiss him, delighting in her new freedom to do so. 'I'll be fine. Don't kill the contractors, will you?'

'If I'm merciful, they'll have you to thank. Off you go.'

She walked quickly down the passage to her own room and sat on the undisturbed bed, clutching his robe around her and wondering what she had done. She had a lover. Memories of the night and his tender care for her made her blood sing. How could anything so wonderful be a mistake? She could at least live on the hope that she must mean something to him: the pleasures of the night had not been one-sided, after all. She fell back on to the bed, her body relaxed, not sleeping, but allowing her mind to drift and dwell on Ross and all she knew of him.

She surfaced hours later, knowing that she had to face a house empty of Ross and full of all the speculations of those who were still here. She realised she had dozed still wearing his robe and shed it reluctantly, deciding not to return it until he came for it himself. To her imagination it held the warmth of his body.

Downstairs there was no sign of anyone, but she heard the sound of the typewriter from Miss Johnson's office. She hesitated for a moment and then shrugged; she had to face people some time. She knocked on the door and went in. The secretary looked up.

'Good morning, Miss Morris. Did you enjoy the dance?'

She hardly remembered it, but she smiled, 'I had a marvellous time,' she said honestly.

'No trouble with that fastening?'

'None.' After all, Ross had not found it so difficult. There was a kind of secret delight in this sort of conversation, but it had its dangers. She suddenly realised that half of her longed to tell the secretary the truth. And that, she knew, would not be a good idea.

'I just wanted to thank you again for your help.'

'It was no trouble,' the other woman smiled. 'I'm surprised you've got the energy to work this morning.' She seemed to approve, so Olivia said nothing to disillusion her. 'Miss Stephens is not yet down,' she added in a voice whose lack of comment was expressive.

'I'm running late myself, I'd better get on,' Olivia said, and made her way to the library.

Bar the door and go to sleep, he had advised. It was an attractive prospect in some ways, if only because it was his suggestion, but a couch of dusty books and boxes had little real appeal. She looked around the room, becoming aware of how nearly her job was over. Most of the shelves were empty, their contents catalogued and classified and stored in labelled boxes. Little remained beyond one small bay and the three boxes of books to be sent for repair and the one large box that held material on which she needed further information and advice.

Perhaps she should have gone to London with him. Professionally it was the obvious thing to do, and she would have to consult someone there, or possibly in Oxford, soon. But if she had gone with him today she could not delude herself into thinking it would have been for any but the most private of reasons. She looked around the room again, its emptiness seeming to mock her. Did that one small bay represent the limit of time available to them, or would he expect her to stay on when she had finished, and ignore the comments and glances of the others as they became aware of her changed status? She would be intimate with him in one way, but an outsider in everything else that was important.

She sat down. The doubts that she had intended to ignore in favour of memories would not after all be suppressed. She realised they were not really doubts: she knew for certain that there was no way she could stay on at the house just as his lover, or mistress, or whatever the right word was. She had too much pride, and was too greedy to share the rest of Ross's life.

For a moment she toyed with the idea that he might want more of her—if not marriage, then at least they might live together. But common sense could not sustain that dream. If she was honest she knew that it was marriage she wanted: an acknowledged right to share his life and eventually to bear his children. And he had never pretended that was on offer.

'It will be easier to seduce you if we're living together.' He had been teasing, deliberately trying to shock, but there had been an element of truth there, too—a warning of the limitations of his intentions, and she had accepted those limitations when she had gone into his arms last night. She could not change the rules now.

She had begun to work in a desultory sort of way, filing some cards and sorting others, when she heard the doors open. Idiotic anticipation flared up and died instantly as she turned to see Theresa in the doorway.

'Yes?' she asked. The blonde woman did not often intrude on her territory.

'I just wondered how you were getting on.' The pale blue eyes were watching Olivia intently. Was she looking for signs of passion, or tears? Uneasily aware that both might be visible, she pushed her glasses up the bridge of her nose and indicated the emptying shelves.

'Not badly, as you can see.'

'You've nearly finished?' There was satisfaction as well as a question in the light voice.

'Nearly.' Olivia was cautious.

'You were very lucky that Ross took you on, weren't you?'

That had no power to hurt, it was so evidently true. 'Very,' she agreed. 'It's been a marvellous experience.'

She had meant the comment quite simply as a reference to her work, but the other woman's suspicions clearly read another meaning into it. 'You left the dance early, didn't you?' she challenged.

'Just before midnight.' It was surprising how easy it was not to respond to this attack. 'Did you enjoy yourself?' she asked politely.

'Not much. I don't like these country gatherings of farmers' wives. But you have to mix with these people when they're so interested in your work. It's only professional.'

It didn't sound like an adequate reason for going to a ball, thought Olivia. Was it her own failure to mix with the crowd or her unprofessionalism at leaving early that was being commented on? She could not rouse much indignation. 'I enjoyed it,' she said mildly.

'I'm sure you did.' This time the dislike was unveiled. 'You clung to Ross as though you owned him, and then dragged him away as soon as you thought no one was watching.' The sharp eyes demanded to know what else had happened that evening. Silence was the easiest defence. It seemed only to infuriate Theresa. 'I've been watching you since you arrived,' she told Olivia. 'The poor defenceless orphan appealing to Ross's generosity. Very clever of you, indeed. He doesn't often fall for such an obvious line, but most men are fools at times. He must have seen you as some sort of charity case.' Her expressive glance said, quite clearly, that no one could find any other appeal in such a plain face and figure. Despite herself, Olivia flushed.

'I've done the job I was employed to do,' she said as evenly as she could. 'My home background has nothing to do with my ability.'

'But it's a damn good way of getting someone's sympathy. Still, you won't be around much longer, will you?' It was a challenge as well as a sneer.

'I don't know,' she said deliberately. 'Ross has offered me a permanent job with Design House.'

Theresa's astonishment and fury were satisfyingly evident. 'What do you mean?' she demanded. 'There's never been any call for your sort of stuff in the firm,' she said with contempt.

'Apparently Ross thinks there is. He was most insistent.'

'I don't believe you.' But there was uncertainty in her voice and Olivia knew she did.

'Ask him,' she shrugged, and then suddenly tired of the game of half-truths that her pride had started. 'Now, if you'll excuse me, I've work to do.' She turned away and heard the doors slam.

Theresa would know soon enough that she had no need to fear her continued presence, and the petty triumph of even temporarily upsetting her rival soon faded. She knew she had been right to refuse the job: the time would inevitably come when she would have to get away fast, and the easier that would be, the better.

The encounter left an unpleasant taste behind. Contempt was hard to ignore and some of Theresa's words had had barbs that were not easily dislodged. The suspicion that she was indeed a 'charity case' and that Ross's attraction had some foundation in curiosity and pity was not new. Theresa had only revived doubts that were already there.

Wearily she turned back to the filing cards. She should have gone to London. Theresa might not know, but she certainly suspected, and already her poison was working. In London at least she would have had a day or two longer before their private world was soiled by speculation. Half of her longed for Ross so that she could be reassured in his arms; half of her dreaded his return, knowing that she could not, and he would not, hide what had happened between them. If ever she had thought there might be something romantic in 'having an affair' she was learning too quickly about its tawdry side.

Facing Patrick was as hard as meeting Theresa. They were all together at lunch and Theresa had clearly decided that patronising her was the most effective weapon.

'I'm sure you must have found lots of interesting books in the library,' she said.

'A few,' agreed Olivia.'

'Are any of them of any value?'

'They may be. I want to check some details with other authorities,' she said.

'Of course. I keep forgetting how inexperienced you are.' The sweet tones reduced Olivia's skills to those of a filing clerk. Patrick glanced sharply at her.

'I'm sure Olivia knows exactly what she's doing,' he said, and firmly changed the subject, beginning to talk about the dance in a deliberate attempt to make them all laugh. 'Val terrifies me,' he said. 'She tore me away from Theresa and thrust me defenceless into a gaggle of beautiful debutantes who kept forcing champagne down me and insisting I explore the remoter regions of the garden.' He mopped a fevered brow. 'I barely escaped uncompromised, I assure you. A man has his reputation to think of, after all.'

And a woman can lose hers without a struggle. Patrick's humour was entertaining, but it seemed slightly forced. When she had seen him first that day he had looked at her with something like concern or sadness, and she couldn't help remembering Ross's comment that he was half in love with her. Whether there was any truth or not in that, he was still obviously making himself her defender against Theresa. It was a relief to return to work.

She thought about skipping dinner altogether, but that would only confirm people's suspicions. She joined the others without much appetite. Half-way through the meal the telephone rang and Miss Johnson automatically left to answer it. She came back a few minutes later.

'Mr Courtenay would like a word about the books you wanted checked,' she said to Olivia.

There were no books. She wondered if everyone else at the table knew that it was only an excuse. Perhaps not Miss Johnson, although one never knew with her, but Theresa was looking furious and Patrick thoughtful. She left the room not knowing whether to be embarrassed or delighted by his call.

She picked up the receiver. 'Hello?' She felt absurdly shy.

'Have I compromised you?' His soft laugh did more than anything else could have done to restore her balance.

'Thoroughly.'

'Good.' There was a very male satisfaction in his voice. He went on more sympathetically, 'An awkward meal?'

'Not at all,' she managed to say. 'Theresa's trying to kill me with a glance, Patrick is feeling sorry for me and even Miss Johnson's beginning to wonder. I haven't seen Joe today because, for some unaccountable reason, I got up late, but he's probably got his own ideas too.' Somehow it was easier to joke and put everything back in proportion now that she had this fragile link with him.

'I'll be back tomorrow evening,' he said. 'Can you brave it out till then, or do you want to join me here?'

She hesitated. It would be almost an open declaration, but that already seemed irrelevant. It also seemed too like running away and she did not want to do that.

'I'll survive. I've plenty of work to do and I think Theresa's spending most of tomorrow at Lady Rushton's.' She had at last begun to concentrate on the commission she detested.

'If you're sure?'

'I'm certain.'

'Well, go to bed early and substitute my bathrobe for that turquoise thing you were wearing the other night and try to imagine I'm holding you.'

Her body quickened in unconscious response to the image he created. She heard his chuckle, as though he could sense her reaction and was pleased by it.

'I have to go,' she said quickly. She wondered how much her face would reveal when she went back to the others.

'I know. I just don't want you to. I needed to hear your voice.'

That he could need as well as want her was the most important thing he could have said. 'I need you too,' she admitted. There was a pause.

'I'm going to say goodbye. If this call goes on any longer I'll be tearing down to Wiltshire tonight to abduct you. Goodnight, love. I hope you sleep as badly as I will.'

'Goodnight.' She heard him replace the receiver. She held hers a moment longer, listening to the hum on the empty line, and then, reluctantly, replaced it.

She walked slowly back to the dining-room. An animated discussion seemed to be going on there and she did not want to face the edged exchanges that made up so much of the conversation when Ross was away. She hesitated at the door and heard Miss Johnson's cool tones.

'I don't see that it's any concern of ours.'

'It is if an incompetent and scheming girl can get a place in the firm.' That was Theresa's voice, shrill with indignation. 'It's bad enough down here, but it's his own house and he can make a fool of himself if he chooses, but he can't make a fool of the firm's reputation.'

She had known when she told her of his offer that it was a mistake. Pride could be too expensive.

'Ross is no fool, in business or private,' Patrick said, anger in his voice.

'Then why this sudden passion,' there was an unmistakable sneer on that word, 'for old books?'

'I don't think we're in any position to judge Mr Courtenay's actions,' said Miss Johnson firmly. 'Nor do you have any proof of your accusations.'

'She's jealous,' said Patrick flatly.

'And if I am, it's because I've every reason to be. I can't bear to see someone like Ross losing his dignity and judgement over some . . .'

'Stop it.' There was authority in Miss Johnson's voice. 'This is getting you nowhere and she will be back in a moment. I suggest we change the subject and forget this one.'

They might do the former, but not the latter. Olivia listened to the silence for about a minute longer, feeling slightly sick, and then quietly opened the dining-room door.

CHAPTER EIGHT

OLIVIA preferred to try to forget the awkwardness of the rest of that evening. The damage had been done as she stood outside the door, and no hints or evasions could improve or worsen the situation, so she endured it until she could reasonably go to bed without showing any apparent reaction to the atmosphere. When she said goodnight to the others, Miss Johnson's response was warm and Theresa ignored her. Patrick looked as though he wanted to speak to her privately but was stopped by something in her expression. He returned her 'Goodnight,' quietly with a speaking glance at Theresa as he held the door open.

She was glad he had accepted her hint. She didn't want sympathy or reassurance. She didn't even want to admit that she had overheard the conversation, since that would bring up the subject of Ross and herself. If only Patrick knew, none of it mattered anyway since she still had not the slightest intention of accepting the offer of a permanent job. She wanted to be able to get out once it was all over.

What really depressed her was the thought that it might now never get started. How could they have any sort of relationship in this house? And if people other than Theresa suspected that Ross was losing his judgement over her, then she didn't think she could bear it. If Ross was diminishing himself by his affair with her, then she must end things soon.

But not yet. She would see him tomorrow and perhaps all her fears would prove illusions, after all. Remembering his phone call, she lay on the bed wrapped in his robe and tried to shut out the day, recalling only the sound of his voice and what had happened between them the previous night.

It was as she was beginning her examination of the books in the library's final bay next morning that she found something that temporarily drove everything else out of her mind. She had opened the large, anonymous volume and was examining it carefully. At first she thought a sleepless night was making her imaginative, and then she looked more closely and began to wonder. It was a leather-bound book and, like many others in the library, the binding had obviously been commissioned by the owner. She had seen many books devalued by rebinding, but this was was rather different. The contents did not form a 'book' in the accepted sense, and would probably be a nightmare to catalogue: the owner had brought together several articles and short works on related subjects, and it was the substantial last section that intrigued Olivia.

Many people who knew about old books might have missed it, but her wide general knowledge of antiques alerted her. The owner's current interest seemed to be furniture, and she had looked forward to showing this short section to Ross, imagining herself pointing out to him, 'At least one sort of obsession runs in the family.' Now she was holding something altogether more serious. The more she looked at it, the more convinced she was that what she held was a Sheraton pattern-book.

Few had survived. Everyone knew the furniture, but it was as a designer, not a craftsman, that he had made his name, and the few drawings that survived could be traced back to the pattern-books from which the cabinet-makers worked. If this was genuine, it was almost unique in its extent and the degree of its preservation.

Carefully she took detailed notes and shut the volume.

She wanted to rush round the house shouting, 'Look what I've found!' and if Ross had been there she might have done just that. At least here she would not have to explain, even to Theresa, the significance of her find.

She could be wrong. She couldn't believe she was right. She sat for a while and then remembered one of her former lecturers. He had gone on to work at the Victoria and Albert Museum and would either help her or, more likely, put her in touch with someone who could.

It was hard to leave the room in case something happened in her absence, but she reminded herself briskly that the volume had been there since, presumably, Ross's grandfather lost interest in furniture. Where he had first found it, she couldn't imagine.

She knocked on the office door.

'Come in.'

She entered, trying not to wonder if Miss Johnson's attitude had changed towards her.

'Do you mind if I use your phone?' The one in the hall was very public and she didn't want this broadcast until she was more certain. Besides, she wanted Ross to be the first to know.

The secretary looked a little surprised, and then rather formal. 'Of course. Is it private?'

Olivia hesitated. 'Confidential. It's about one of the books in the library.' After Ross's call last night she could not blame the secretary for not believing her. 'You don't have to go,' she said quickly when Miss Johnson stood up.

'I'll leave you in peace. I like a cup of coffee at this time of day anyway. Just give me a call when you're finished.'

Olivia looked at the telephone and smiled wryly. She didn't know Ross's number at either the flat or the studio—it might be difficult to contact him even if that had been her intention.

It did not take long to reach the museum. It took considerably longer to establish who she wanted and for him to be found. Hesitantly she asked in general terms about pattern-books.

'It's a tricky subject,' he told her, 'since they're seldom "books" at all. Who were you thinking of?'

She swallowed. It could do no harm to admit it, she supposed. 'Sheraton.'

There was a long silence. 'If you're serious, and not just guessing, you could be on to something important. Especially if it's more than a couple of pages.'

She thought she heard a faint question in that last statement, but she ignored it. 'Who could tell me a bit more before I get excited and make an idiot of myself?'

'There's a man at the British Library . . .' There was a pause and a rustling of papers, then he gave her a name and phone number. 'Tell him I recommended him,' he suggested.

After a little more conversation Olivia was able to put the phone down and try the new number. Here she was less fortunate. Her contact was out and she could only leave a message, asking him to call her.

She told Miss Johnson she could have her office back, and returned to work feeling slightly dazed. Ever since she had begun this job she had hoped for a significant find, partly as a gesture of thanks for Ross's trust and partly as a signal to all those, including herself, who had doubted her ability. If she was not now completely deluding herself, then what she held in her hands could hardly be more fitting.

Uncertainty, and the knowledge that Ross could not be back before evening, made her unobtrusive for the rest of the day. She seemed almost to feel a waiting calm about the house. She thought of the coming reunion. Her first impulse had been to show him at once what she had found; now she decided to wait until she was just a little more certain. Their meeting tonight would be entirely private and personal.

He had not specified a time for his return, and she found anticipation growing from late afternoon onwards. When dinner time arrived and he had not returned, she had little appetite and later Patrick beat her easily at chess for the first time.

'You're not concentrating,' he accused.

'Sorry.'

He looked down at the small red queen in his hand and back up at her. 'Are you unhappy?' he asked quietly.

She was startled. 'Do I look it?'

'No,' he hesitated. 'Remote and rather keyed up, I suppose. Olivia,' he seemed to search for words, aware of the others in the room, then he went on at last, 'if you ever *are* unhappy, you will treat me as a friend, won't you?'

Touched, she smiled wryly, accepting his doubts about her relationship with Ross as well as his kindness. 'Thanks. I'll remember that.' She might well need a friend before long, but not if it meant driving a wedge between Ross and Patrick.

Eleven o'clock came and went. He must have had to spend the night in town, after all. She went up to bed, disappointed with him for not phoning and annoyed with herself at such possessiveness.

She was in bed, the small light on the table beside her the only illumination, when she heard the quiet knock and the turning of the door-handle. She put down the book she had been failing to read and looked up.

Dark blue eyes regarded her, smiling slightly as he saw the robe she had wrapped round herself although the night was not cold. He still wore his black leather jacket over jeans and a dark shirt, and the freshness of the night air was about him as he stooped over the bed to accept the mouth she turned up towards him.

He sat on the bed, pulling her more fully into his embrace, finally breaking off the kiss to enfold her tightly in his arms, burying his face in her hair. The texture and smell of leather against her cheek, the feel of his shirt against his back where her hands were beneath the jacket, were intimate and exciting. He had come to her before anyone else and that was all that mattered.

The first intensity passed. She drew back to look up into his face as he smiled at her. There were lines of tiredness around his eyes, and she longed to make them disappear.

'Hard day at the office?' she tried.

He laughed, shrugging off his jacket. 'Foul. Nobody understands me,' he added with a plaintive sigh.

'I'm not surprised.' She knew she didn't. 'I didn't think you would get back tonight,' she added despite herself.

He was idly coiling a lock of her hair around one finger. The gentle touch was having an unsettling effect on her and she wanted to draw him down so that he was cradled against her, but she sensed his restlessness.

'I nearly didn't. Every time I thought things were under control someone found a new problem to worry about. I felt like a mother duck trying to abandon her brood. You're lucky I didn't come in here quacking.'

'You're lucky I like ducks. And I'm glad you came in.'

He touched the neck of the robe she wore. 'So am I. I won't stay, I'm too tired to do you justice and the house seems like Piccadilly Circus for some reason. I just wanted a few minutes' peace. I've been dreaming of holding you all day, and the thought has kept me sane for the last fifty miles, despite a conspiracy by someone to dig up every road in the county.' Exasperation and something else mingled in his voice, but he was beginning to relax.

'Then why are you sitting there at arm's length?' she asked mildly.

'Heaven knows.' He reached out and took her in his arms, kicking off his shoes and stretching out on the bed beside her. 'That's better.' He kissed her lightly, running his fingers through the length of her hair. 'You know,' he said, finding the sash at her waist, 'you don't really need this now I'm here.'

'So I don't.' She lifted slightly to let him remove the sash and part the robe. She wore nothing beneath it.

'I don't think,' he said after a moment, his hand beginning to trail across her skin, 'that I'm ever going to feel quite the same about this garment again.' He yawned and drew her closer to him, and then turned so that his head lay against her breasts. 'Suddenly nothing is so trying any more,' he admitted. 'Now you tell me what a horrid time you've had without me and I'll comfort you.'

She thought of the past day and a half. There was no point in mentioning all her own inner doubts, and she certainly wasn't going to say anything about the overheard conversation. She brushed the heavy dark hair back from his forehead. 'No problems, I'm afraid,' she told him.

He lifted his head and looked at her. 'Liar.' His voice was quiet but serious. 'Don't shut me out, Olivia. Has Theresa been impossible? Do you want me to get rid of her?'

'No!' If she needed confirmation that the other woman was right, it was in this lightly worded suggestion that he should sack a skilled employee just to protect her. She saw his quick frown at her sharp reaction. 'No,' she repeated more calmly. 'Nothing's happened that I can't cope with.

And you're back.' At the moment that was all that was important. She realised then that, even if she had not already made up her mind, she would not have told him of her find tonight. These moments were too intimate and personal.

'Yes, I'm home.' She couldn't tell whether he was talking about the house or his head against her breasts. He yawned again. 'What we ought to be doing is curling up together so that I can have the delight of waking you in a few hours with all manner of improper suggestions.' He chuckled as he observed the evident effect of his words upon her. 'Instead, I am going to kiss you,' his lips teased the tip of each breast before brushing her mouth, 'and hold you tightly for a minute or two more, and then I am going to sneak along the corridors of my own home like a naughty schoolboy,' he ended between amusement and exasperation.

He tightened his clasp on her, drawing her naked body against him so that she could feel his arousal. She had learned something even in the one night they had spent together, and she arched her hips into his in deliberate provocation.

'Witch,' he growled, holding her close. 'I want you, but I want more than a furtive night or two.' Despite the demands of his body, his voice was serious. 'As soon as I can arrange it, you and I are going away together, and I doubt if we'll get out of bed for a week. So don't say you weren't warned.'

He sat up as he spoke, holding her down by the shoulders when she would have clung to him. 'No, lie still. That's the picture of you I want to sleep with if I can't have the real thing.' The robe hung wide and her body was open to his touch. He bent and kissed her quickly. 'Tomorrow we *will* get round to talking. Now I'm going to find Patrick if he's still awake. I've a lot of work for him,' he sounded vaguely pleased at the thought, 'and then I am going to bed. To *try* to sleep,' he added with a mock frown at her blatant invitation. Then he had gone.

She wished he had stayed. She should have told him she didn't mind the gossip. Time was suddenly very short, but it was too late. She drew his robe protectively round her and made her own attempt to sleep.

For the first time in two days she woke feeling full of energy and eager for an early walk. The sunny spell had given way to more overcast weather, but it was still dry and, although some of the roses were blown and dropping, their colours still rioted. Joe had welcomed her in the mornings as a sort of junior colleague since the morning after the storm.

'Morning, miss.'

'Morning, Joe.'

'Need some more rain, we do.' He squinted up at the sky without much hope and went back to work.

There was still some time before she need begin the day's work, concentrating on routine tasks while awaiting the phone call from the British Library and trying to ignore her body's awareness of Ross's presence not far away. She went over to a low stone wall by a raised bed to sit and soak up the morning air. It was here that Ross found her.

He stood looking at the tall, slender figure in old jeans and a T-shirt for a few moments, a slightly brooding expression on his face, but it lightened into a smile as she looked up.

Her stomach seemed to dissolve. It was almost humiliating that a smile and a lifted eyebrow could make her feel so helplessly weak. She tried to sound self-possessed.

'Hello. Did you sleep well?'

He sat beside her, not quite touching her. 'Of course not. And I hope you didn't either.'

'I'm sorry. I slept wonderfully.' It was true, and she giggled at his look of indignation.

'I hope you dreamed of me.' She was about to reply when he added softly, 'And if you dare say "no" I shall use this aptly named bed to persuade you that you should give more attention to the subject.'

She blushed, almost annoyed that he could still make her colour so easily. 'In that case I'm very tempted to say "no",' she managed to say defiantly.

'Liar.' He chuckled. 'This is altogether too public for what I have in mind—and if I touch you I just might not be able to stop,' he added, sounding half surprised at his own feelings.

'Then I'd better get off to work and save you from yourself,' she said, standing up and brushing off her jeans.

'Don't go for a minute.' She sat down again. 'How long before you've emptied the shelves and I can send the painters in?' he asked.

She thought about it. There was still work to be done on a number of books, not to mention yesterday's find, but they could easily be moved to another room. Clearing the final bay and cataloguing its more straightforward contents should not take long.

'Three days?' she suggested.

'Good. That gives me time to tidy up the loose ends of the London chaos and break it to Patrick that he can stop lotus-eating here and take over in town while I have a holiday. Then we can have some time to ourselves wherever you want. We could throw everyone out and stay here; I could show you the etchings in my flat as I once promised you,' he flickered a sidelong smile at her, 'or we could take off for some far-flung but reasonably comfortable corner of the globe. If globes have corners,' he added thoughtfully.

'It sounds wonderful.' She could not quite keep a wistful note from her voice.

He was watching her closely. 'You decide,' he told her. 'You've three days to think about it. It'll give you something to look forward to when life—or Theresa—seems most irritating.' He seemed to make up his mind about something then, and went on deliberately, still studying her reaction, 'And I'll look round for a project that we can both work on if ever we decide to come back to earth.'

His close regard had given her some warning. She couldn't quite stop herself fiddling with her glasses, but she managed to meet his gaze with apparent determination.

'No, Ross.'

'What do you mean "no"?'

'Just what I said. I told you before that I wasn't going to accept a permanent job with you, and I haven't changed my mind.'

There was something steely in his look and he was very still. She wanted to get away, but forced herself not to flinch when he said quietly, with a sort of controlled reasonableness, 'Why?'

'Because whatever's happening between us on a personal level doesn't affect my ideas about my work.' He didn't believe her, and she couldn't entirely blame him since her original rejection of the job had been for personal, not professional reasons. She could only hope he didn't realise this.

'You intend to disappear abroad or to whatever obscure job you find in the "situations vacant" column as soon as possible?' he asked, the tone of mild enquiry somehow more intimidating than overt anger.

'I'm not rushing off,' she tried to protest. 'You know I've got a month or two before I have to make any decisions after I finish here.'

'So that's what you're giving us, is it? A month or two?

What do you plan? A flat somewhere where I can drop in and visit you whenever's suitable? Or were you intending to stay on here as a sort of mistress in residence?'

'I don't know! I haven't thought about it. We've only——'

'We've only made love once,' he interrupted, anger making the words brutal. 'And already you're planning the end of it. It seems to me that you've given it far more thought than I have. Perhaps you'll let me know exactly what you expect to happen?'

He stood up and she knew she must have gone white. His sudden fury made her feel sick; she had expected him to be annoyed by her stubbornness, but this was far worse than she had ever imagined possible. She drew back quickly when he put out his hand and his expression changed.

'Olivia——' he began, and then stopped.

A tall figure was striding across the lawn towards them, waving in greeting. It was Val Standish.

'Ross!' she called.

He straightened, swearing beneath his breath, and moved so that he masked her from Val's sight for a moment. She buried her head in her hands and wondered how quickly she could get away.

'Hello, Val.' He sounded resigned.

She kissed her brother on the cheek. 'I thought I'd managed to catch you if I came out early,' she said with satisfaction.

'You sound like Uncle Hubert. What do you want?'

'A chat. And I wanted to meet Olivia again.'

That was a pity. She had hoped to slip away after the briefest of greetings, and had already stood up and moved a pace or two away, as if to leave brother and sister alone together. Without seeming to watch her, Ross evidently noticed her move, because he reached out and snared her wrist with fingers that felt cold. She remembered the velvet band with the orchid on it, and the kiss he had put in its place, and couldn't quite suppress a shiver. His grip tightened fractionally.

'Here she is. We were going to fortify ourselves with coffee. I suppose you want some, too?'

'Put like that, how could I refuse?' Sharp eyes were looking from Ross to Olivia as though wondering exactly what she had interrupted. Olivia had the uncomfortable feeling that those eyes saw entirely too much, and tried again to pull away.

'I've got to get on with my work,' she protested. Ross did not let go. Brown eyes watching them seemed both curious and amused.

'I'm sure you can have coffee if the boss orders it, can't she?'

'She can. It'll do her good. She needs something to clear her mind about her work,' he agreed a trifle grimly, and although he slackened his grip on her wrist there seemed no way she could simply obey her instinct to turn and run. Besides, what good would it do? She had no transport, and everything here was his. Their confrontation had been delayed by Val's appearance, not ended.

She walked back to the house with them, responding as politely as she could to Val's conversation while hardly hearing a word.

Ross poured coffee for them all and fielded most of Val's questions, but his sister was not easily deterred.

'Did you enjoy the dance?' she asked Olivia.

'You know what I think of your mass gatherings,' Ross told her.

'That's why I'm not asking you.'

Olivia fiddled with her cup. Why did everyone ask this question, with all its attendant memories? 'Very much indeed,' she said quietly, avoiding the mockery she knew she would see on Ross's face. 'It was kind of you to invite me.'

'Nonsense, I'm glad you could come. I'd already heard about Ross's new discovery, and not just from him,' she added before he could comment, 'and I wanted to meet you.'

'Curiosity is very vulgar,' he pointed out.

'So I'm always being told,' his sister replied without offence. She turned back to Olivia. 'I gather this is your first freelance job?'

Who was the other source of information about her? Theresa? Probably. 'Yes. I used to work with my father.' She explained about the shop.

'It must be quite a contrast doing this sort of thing?'

Was that a sneer, as Theresa would have made it? No, she seemed interested. 'Yes, but I've enjoyed it.' She would not look at Ross and wished the subject would change. But Val was persistent.

'I'm not sure I would have done,' she commented, glancing at her brother. 'At least in the shop you were your own boss. It can't be so satisfying to be employed by someone else. Don't you feel you've lost your independence?'

Only emotionally. If only she knew how much the opposite was true about her work. She was no longer tied to a failing business and was being given every chance to develop her talents. But Ross was looking as though this point of view was new to him, and it might be better not to protest too openly about it.

'It's very different,' she said. 'I'm not sure you can compare them at all.' She drained her cup and stood up before Val could think of her next question. 'But I really do have to get on now, if you'll excuse me?'

Ross had stood when she did, and for one moment she thought he was going to follow her, but Val prevented him.

'I wanted to ask you about an idea I had of extending the drawing-room,' she told him, and he had to stay.

'We'll talk again later,' he promised Olivia as he held the door for her.

He seemed to have controlled the worst of his anger, but she closed the library doors behind her with the relief of one finding sanctuary, however temporary. She sat down heavily at the wide desk and stared at the brown calf-bound folio in front of her. It was beginning to seem like the only good thing that could come out of this mess.

When they were alone together, with no thoughts of past or future or the outside world, then things had seemed perfect between herself and Ross. But life wasn't like that, and it was probably already too late to recapture that idyll. So what could she do? She could give in and take the job, and all that it entailed of working with him without betraying the extent of her feelings; or she could pretend to accept the idea of the job until the affair was over. But she was not sure how well she could deceive him, or if she wanted to.

She could, of course, simply say, 'I love you and I want to be with you always,' but she did not think she could bear his rejection. And his kindness would be even worse. The hope that she might get neither reaction flickered and died. Life wasn't that sort of fairy-tale.

She brushed her hand over the leather in front of her. It was soft to the touch, only a little brittle and flaking on the hinges and spine. She had found it with such high hopes and now, even if she went straight to him with it, it would seem almost like a plea for his favour. 'Look what I've found.

Won't you accept it and forget you're angry with me?' She didn't want it to be like that. She had wanted him simply to share her delight in its discovery.

What she really wanted, she decided, was to get away. Not necessarily for ever, though he might not want her to come back, but just for long enough to find some sort of perspective on what was happening to her. For twenty-three years her life had been ordinary and safe; it might also have been occasionally boring and frustrating, but nothing in it had prepared her for the emotions of the past few months.

Jeremy's defection had never really mattered much; he had probably only saved her from having to reject him. Knowing what she did now, the thought that she might have just drifted into marriage with him because it was expected of her was appalling. But she thought it would probably never have happened. Her father's death had undermined the fabric of her life and was still a fresh wound. His loss meant the end of all that was familiar in her life, and her growing awareness of how narrow it had been. It was Ross who had shown her how it might be filled in an undreamed of way, and made her want a future that she had never known could exist.

She was still looking blankly at the book in front of her, and had made no move to begin work when a sharp knock at the door was followed immediately by its opening.

She hardly had time to brace herself for whatever Ross was going to say when his sister shut the door behind her and came over to the desk.

Olivia looked up, not bothering to hide the lack of welcome in her eyes. The other woman pulled out a chair and sat down opposite her, her smile disturbingly like her brother's.

'You look,' she remarked, 'as though you'd much rather today had never begun.'

Despite herself, Olivia laughed. 'The first hour and a half were quite enjoyable,' she admitted.

'Is it any comfort if I say Ross is in the same state?'

She thought about it. 'No, not really,' she decided.

'Would it help if I got rid of him for a while?'

'Could you?' Olivia was fascinated.

'Possibly not if he didn't want me to. But he just might take the excuse if I offer it.'

It would solve nothing, of course, but she was in that state of mind when even a temporary reprieve was welcome. She didn't have to say anything. Val was already standing up again.

'Right. My brother is about to give me free professional advice about some alterations I have no intention of making. Charles will want him to stay to lunch and discuss the state of the country, but I can't promise much beyond that. I'll be seeing you again,' she finished, and left the room.

It might have sounded like a warning, but Olivia had the feeling that, improbably, she had found a friend. She would have liked to have talked to Val and asked her why she wanted to help, but at least she had a few hours in which to prepare herself to see Ross again. Instead, she put her head down on the soft calfskin and closed her eyes.

CHAPTER NINE

SLEEP cured nothing. She woke with a stiff neck and a slight headache, and the suspicion that it would have been better not to have put off whatever Ross was going to say to her. She wondered what time it was and how much was left to her. As a child, watching romantic old films of aristocrats going to the scaffold, she had wondered at the courage of people who went unhesitatingly to their fate. Now she knew. It wasn't courage, after all: they just wanted to get it over with.

A gong rang in the hall. Lunch. There were too many meals, too many hours of polite conversation and underlying speculation; but avoiding them made the next one even worse. She stood up and left the library.

Miss Johnson's presence meant that conversation was mainly neutral, although Theresa's eyes were busy and Patrick's concerned. She wondered exactly what showed on her face, and wondered too how they would react if she said, quite calmly, 'Yes, we're lovers. Yes, he wants me to work for him, and no, I don't intend to. And you have raised doubts that, you'll be glad to know, make it impossible for me to change my mind.'

But naturally she said no such thing. She turned instead to Miss Johnson.

'I'm expecting a phone call some time today. I'm sorry I had to give your number, but do you think you could call me if it comes through?'

'Of course,' the secretary agreed.

'From the Cotswold boyfriend?' suggested Theresa. 'I'm glad to see you're keeping your options open. After all, you'll have to recognise your limitations some time, won't you?'

It was all too much. She pushed aside her untouched plate and stood up, overrriding Patrick's furious exclamation.

'It's about time you recognised yours, isn't it, Theresa? At least I seem to have made more progress in a couple of weeks than you have in the months you've been trying.'

She walked out of the room with a slightly grim feeling of satisfaction.

She would not stay in this house any longer, even if she had to walk to the station. She went quickly back to her room and threw a change of clothes and her washing things into a small bag that would not be too heavy to carry. She had locked the bedroom door and was glad of it when she heard a knock. Patrick's voice called to her.

'Olivia? Are you all right?'

'I will be. Just leave me alone for a while,' she called back without opening the door. Adding, 'Please, Patrick?' when she sensed that he had not gone.

'OK.' He sounded reluctant. 'But I won't be far away if you want me.'

She held her breath till she was sure he had gone and then returned to her preparations, conscious of time passing. She had to leave some message for Ross, and that would not be easy. Best perhaps just to write it without planning or trying to work out how he was going to react.

She found a pen and a sheet of paper and hesitated a moment before she began, and then wrote quickly to get it over with.

'Dear Ross,' she started, 'I need time to think. I'll contact you in a few days and come back if you want me to. There's not much work left to be done and I'm sure you can easily find someone far more competent than me to take over. The only really important thing is the folio on the library desk.'

She explained what she thought might be in the book, and about the phone call that should come that afternoon. Then she wondered what else to say. The facts about work had been easy. How did you write about emotions? In the end she scrawled a few words quickly, hardly thinking.

'I'm sorry I seem to be running away,' she wrote. 'Perhaps I'm not mature enough to cope, after all. Thank you for everything. Olivia.'

She had though of signing herself 'Cinderella', but that belonged to the fairy-tale world where everyone lived happily ever after. She read the note again. It was curt and clumsy and inadequate, especially that last paragraph, but it seemed that, with emotions, if you couldn't pour out the truth, there wasn't much left to say.

Before she could change her mind she sealed it and wrote his name clearly on the envelope. She propped it on the dressing-table. It might be a few hours before he found it, but that was so much the better.

Hearing no sound in the passage, she slipped out of her room with her bag. Her first thought had been to cross the gardens and leave by the back gate, hoping to get a lift once she got out into the narrow lanes. And hoping even more fervently not to meet Ross. Patrick's visit had given her another idea. He had offered help, and surely it could do no harm if he just gave her a lift to the station? Ross might be angry for a while, but he could not really blame Patrick. She hoped she could find him, and not Theresa. There was little time to spare for searching.

She was in the dining-room when she heard the car draw up outside. Voices. A woman's voice, and a man's she would have known anywhere in the world, even after the first time she'd heard it as he hauled her to her feet from an icy pavement. Val hadn't been able to keep him long, then.

The front door opened and there were quick steps across the hallway. She heard the library door open and then slam shut. The footsteps were coming in this direction, and she had her fingers on the handle of the french window when she heard Theresa's voice just outside.

'Ross?' she asked plaintively.

'Yes? What is it? Have you seen Olivia?' He sounded impatient.

She could almost see the expressive shrug. 'No. I think she's upstairs. Could I have a word with you?'

There was no time to hear Ross's reply. While he was speaking to Theresa he was not searching for her, that was all that mattered. She turned the handle behind her and stepped quietly out on to the terrace. She might after all have to risk the back way across the gardens, but there was on possibility still left to her. She walked quickly round to the front of the house. Yes. Val's Mini was still there. She had been talking to Joe, but was just getting into the car. Olivia waved urgently.

She must have caught the signal in her mirror because she turned at once and saw Olivia, taking in the bag at a glance. She leaned across and opened the passenger door, starting the engine as soon as Olivia was in.

'Where to?' she asked as though this was some everyday excursion.

'The station, please.' She looked around, feeling both ashamed and triumphant. Joe had seen her, but it might be some time before Ross thought of asking him if he'd seen her, and she didn't see Joe volunteering information unasked.

The little car bounced down the rutted drive until she began to fear that a puncture might end her escapade in farce. Running away was childish enough, without being caught.

They reached the lane safely, however, and she began to relax. She looked across at her driver, who seemed to be concentrating on nothing but the road.

'Thank you very much,' she said, adding, 'but I don't understand why you're doing this for me.'

She received a quick glance from those clear brown eyes. 'Do you have a specific train in mind, or can you spare twenty minutes? There's a lay-by just ahead,' she said instead of answering directly.

It seemed a small enough request, and she had no idea of the train timetable. 'I can spare the time, but I'd rather the car couldn't be seen by anyone happening to pass,' she agreed cautiously.

'And Ross just might take it into his head to act faster than you hope,' Val commented. 'So why don't I take a detour in the wrong direction and then if he *does* get to the station it'll be before us and he may even think he's on the wrong trail?'

Despite herself, Olivia had to laugh at the satisfaction in the other woman's face. 'You sound like someone in a spy movie,' she accused. 'All right, let's take a detour.'

The little car took a sharp left turn and began to wind slowly through narrow lanes that Olivia never afterwards remembered clearly.

'Why am I doing this?' Val repeated Olivia's question. 'I'm not altogether sure, although I hope I'd do the same for anyone who looked as desperate as you did when you came round the corner of the house just now.'

'That can't be all. You were kind earlier.'

'Interfering is what Ross would call it. It's what he *did* call it, in fact, when I asked about you this morning.' She sounded amused rather than offended. 'I suppose you guessed that Theresa managed to fill me in with all sorts of grisly details about your scheming plots?'

'I thought it must be her.'

'Well, that naturally predisposed me in your favour.'

'Naturally?'

'Yes. She was divorced about a year ago and has been hanging around Ross like a female spider ever since.' It was oddly cheering to contemplate a cartoon spider with Theresa's pretty face and blonde hair. 'I don't think he'd ever do anything drastic like marrying her, although I did think once he might take advantage of what was being so blatantly offered,' she continued. 'Fortunately Uncle Hubert died and he inherited The Folly and that kept him busy, and the boredom that was setting in in London began to recede.' She glanced over at Olivia. 'You won't be upset if I point out that female company has never been much of a problem for him?'

'Anything else would surprise me,' she admitted. 'It's one reason . . .'

'Why you've got so many doubts at the moment? I'm not surprised. Don't worry. If he's serious, he won't let a little set-back like this stop him. It might be just what he needs, in fact.'

'I still don't understand why you're supporting me against him.' Another thought occurred to her, and Val picked up her sudden doubt before she could say anything. In some ways she was as quick as her brother.

'Or am I just being a devious and manipulating big sister and ridding him of a complication I disapprove of?' She laughed. 'I value my neck too much for that. Sisterhood and five years' seniority wouldn't save me—and quite rightly. No, but I do think he's put you in an impossible position in that house while Theresa's still there. He knows she's jealous and bitchy, but I don't think he's ever seen quite how nasty she can be nor, to do him justice, does he realise quite how obsessed she is. He's not that conceited. She came to see me a couple of days ago,' she finished, remembering.

'About me?'

'About you.' Val seemed to find the memory distasteful. 'Basically to tell me that you were an undesirable influence who was corrupting his judgement. And I simply didn't believe it. I have, after all, known him considerably longer than she has. But it finally reminded me of when I'd first heard him speak about you. At least, I assume it was you.'

'When was that?' There was a curiously guilty luxury in talking about Ross to someone who knew him well, even when she was trying to escape from him.

'January.' She saw she didn't need to elaborate and went on, 'He came back from Gloucestershire with three very attractive pieces of furniture and in an extremely odd state of mind. He's not often given to depression, but he was certainly very fed up about something, almost bitter. He virtually gave up work on the house for a while. I finally asked him flat out what was wrong, and he stared hard at me and I thought he was going to tell me to shut up, but he didn't.'

'What did he say?' This hardly sounded like Ross.

'Not much. He shrugged, and said, "Usual movie plot, I suppose: right girl engaged to wrong man." Then he offered me a drink, and even I know when the time really has come to keep quiet.'

For a moment, Olivia's dreams came alive and she almost

asked Val to turn the car round. Then memories of the more recent past returned. 'He got over it,' she said.

'I thought so. But Miss Johnson had very strict orders to pass on anything that came in from your father, I gather. And then you came. I was a bit slow, I'm afraid. It took Theresa's comments, on top of Ross's lack of any, before I put two and two together.'

'The total's still five, I'm afraid.' She didn't dare take the chance on anything else, the disillusion would be so great that it was easier not to hope. And she still had to get away.

Val looked sceptical, but did not try to argue. 'Ross can look after himself, I suppose, and deal with Theresa into the bargain. I don't like the idea of you as the victim, though. Have you got anywhere to go?' Olivia hesitated. 'I'm not prying—for once—but if you haven't then you can come and stay with me, and neither Charles nor I will say a word to Ross.'

She did not believe for a momeent that such a secret could be kept, but she was touched by the offer. 'Thank you,' she said. 'I'm very grateful, but I do have a place to go to.' But not a person.

'Well, don't tell me where it is.' Olivia had not intended to. 'I'd rather not have to lie to Ross, and he's certain to discover I left you at the station.'

'Don't hang around to see what train I catch,' advised Olivia.

'I won't.' Now there was rueful amusement in her voice. 'I probably ought to go into hiding myself. Can you phone me to let me know you're all right?' she asked more seriously.

Olivia hesitated. 'I'll try, but I won't be on the phone so it may not be possible.'

'I understand. And now we'd better start travelling in the

right direction.' She took a right turn at the next intersection and in a surprisingly short time they were outside the station. Olivia looked around anxiously, but neither the Land Rover nor any other familiar vehicle was in the small car park.

'This is it, I suppose,' she said, and reached for the door-handle. 'Thank you so much for all your help.'

'I'm glad I was around. I'm going to take a very long route home, just in case Ross has decided to wait for me there. Have a good journey, whatever's at the end of it, and please don't drop out of our lives altogether.' Unexpectedly, she leaned across and brushed a quick kiss against Olivia's cheek.

'Thank you,' she said again, touched by the gesture. 'Goodbye.'

She waved as the Mini drove quickly away from the station, and then she went in to the ticket office to find out where the next train was going.

Half an hour later she watched the station disappear from sight behind a bend in the line, and tried to tell herself that she was doing the right thing. She still wasn't sure it was right, all she knew was that it had seemed the only possible thing at the time.

She had been fortunate at the station. The train was a fast one to London and, although Ross could find out without difficulty that she had taken it, since there had been only one other passenger waiting on the platform, he would have no idea where she would go from there. With any luck he would assume she had friends in town with whom she would stay.

She could do that, she supposed, although most of her friends would be more than a little surprised by her unannounced arrival, and might well find it inconvenient. It was not really a plan worth serious consideration. To be a guest in someone else's house when all she wanted was time and peace to restore her self-possession would be folly. No, she had always known where she was going, and she would stay in London only as long as it took to change stations and find a train to Gloucestershire.

It was after ten o'clock at night by the time a taxi dropped her outside the dark and empty windows of her former home. Above the door the white 'For Sale' sign glimmered in the dim street lighting.

'Are you sure this is the right place?' The driver seemed reluctant to abandon her here.

'Yes, quite sure.' She paid him and unlocked the front door, hearing the familiar bell tinkle unexpectedly loudly in the vacant rooms. She had telephoned the estate agent from London to warn him that she would be back in residence for a few days. Now she ought to contact Jeremy just in case someone saw a light and alerted him. First, though, she would look around.

Not quite everything had gone. The fitted carpets were still down in the flat, and in the kitchen there were still a table and two plain chairs. She had packed the crockery and pans away herself before she'd left, and they were all in storage, but a battered kettle still sat on the cooker. In the morning she could buy a mug and whatever basics seemed important. At least the water and electricity were still connected, even though the telephone wasn't.

There were no beds left. She had expected that, but she had also remembered an old mattress bundled under a cover in the attic. With much effort she managed to get it out and into the empty room that had been hers. A couple of old rugs and a dustsheet completed the improvised bed. It was not particularly inviting, but it would do.

Jeremy. She had forgotten him again. It was late, but he

might still be awake. Or out with Susan, of course. She could always leave a message with his mother.

She checked that she had the right change, and walked to the public phone box on the corner. Fortunately the local vandals had not yet got round to wrecking it since it was last repaired. A half-smile touched her lips: there was something to be said for country slowness.

The phone rang half a dozen times, and she began to think there was no one in, then she heard his voice.

'Hello? Jeremy Barker speaking.' She put in the coins as the rapid pips sounded.

'Jeremy? It's Olivia.'

'Olivia!' She could almost see him looking at his watch. 'Why are you ringing from a call box? Is something wrong?'

'No, nothing's wrong.' Nothing she wanted to talk about. 'I just wanted to warn you that I'm back for a few days—I'm phoning from near the shop and I didn't want you to worry if you noticed signs of life.'

'You're at the shop? You can't stay there—there's no furniture or anything!'

For once. 'It's all right. I've got all I need for tonight. 'I'll buy a sleeping-bag or something tomorrow, don't worry,' she tried unsuccessfully to reassure him.

'I don't like it.' He hesitated, and she could guess what he was about to say, and his doubts about Susan's reactions. She was touched when his good nature won the internal debate. 'Look, why don't you come round here for tonight? You know we've got that sofa-bed, and I'm sure Mother would like it.'

Olivia wasn't at all sure, but had no intention of finding out. 'Thanks, but I'd rather be at home, if you don't mind. I want some time to myself.'

He was not particularly sensitive, but he had known her

for some time. 'What's happened?' he asked, sounding angry. 'Has that man upset you?'

Yes, and that's too mild a word for it, but it's nothing you'll ever understand. The words were clear in her mind as she spoke the soothing denials he needed to hear. 'No. It's all right, he's been very kind. I just wanted a break and it took a bit longer than I'd planned to get here.' Wiltshire to Gloucestershire via London was definitely time-consuming.

'Are you sure?' He was calmer now, accepting the situation.

'Quite sure. Goodnight, Jeremy.'

'Goodnight, Olivia. I'll probably drop in some time tomorrow.'

That would give her time to rest and think and find a suitable excuse to calm him again. Some sentimental comment about a few last nights in her old home before it was sold might be as effective as anything.

She stood inside the familiar old place that had been her home for most of her life. It wasn't a home any more, just an empty building waiting for other people to come and make it live with their possessions and thoughts and voices. Without the familiar clutter and, above all, without her father, it was just a rather pleasant shell. There weren't even any ghosts.

Because there seemed nothing else worth doing, she washed quickly in cold water and prepared for bed. With the immersion heater on there would be hot water in the morning.

The dusty rugs and old mattress made her sneeze at first, but they weren't uncomfortable. She sat up in the makeshift bed, propping herself against the wall because she had no pillows. Through the uncurtained window she watched the dark grey summer's night and remembered the day. It was not one she could easily forget: she had probably just ruined her relationship with the man she loved because of a confusion of feelings that she wasn't sure that even she understood.

He did not love her. That had always seemed absolutely self-evident. He had spoken of seduction, teasing her with words and glances and kisses, but never of love. She could believe he liked her; after all, she made him laugh. She knew he desired her. But love? No. And yet she kept coming back to Val's comments with almost wistful longing. 'The right girl.' He could have meant anyone. It was even more likely that he had meant no one, had only been interested in stopping Val's questions. Olivia suspected that Val was a romantic at heart and wanted to see her brother in love, as long as it was with someone she approved of. And it seemed obvious that she was likely to approve of anyone of whom Theresa disapproved. As for Ross wanting to keep in touch with her father, surely that was nothing more than good business practice? Having found a promising supplier, he was certainly not going to ignore him.

It was difficult to tell what comfort or insight the next few days might bring, and she shrank away from the thought of what he would say when she eventually phoned, but she was glad she had run. She loved the old house that had once been Uncle Hubert's treasure chest and Ross was making his own home, but she had been stifled by the others living there and Ross's repeated absences. Theresa had been the worst factor, but the kindness of Miss Johnson and Patrick, their expectation of her hurt, had been almost as bad. And if, on top of everything else, they too saw his feelings for her as an infatuation that was beginning to affect his business sense, then it was past time to leave.

She lay down, hands behind her head, and watched the ceiling. She felt quite relaxed, in a sort of limbo where nothing threatened and decisions could be deferred. Despite scratchy blankets, the hardness of the floor though the thin mattress, and the beginnings of hunger, she was content.

CHAPTER TEN

OLIVIA had no idea of the time when she woke, curled in an uncomfortable huddle in a tangle of dust sheets. All she knew was that it was full daylight and someone was ringing the doorbell.

It had to be Jeremy. The estate agent was the only other person who knew she was there, and he had no reason to contact her. Jeremy must have started to worry again and taken time off to call and reassure himself. She thought without much gratitude of his concern as she struggled to her feet, realising that he was unlikely to go away. If she didn't answer he'd probably come in anyway, since he had a key.

She glanced out of the window. It must be later than she had thought: the town looked quite busy. He was going to be embarrassed when she opened the door in her nightshirt, but that wasn't her problem. The insistent ringing went on. He must be really anxious if he was willing to stand there with his thumb on the bell amid the passers-by.

She walked through the empty shop, her bare feet scuffing the dust on the floorboards. And then she stopped. Outlined against the frosted glass of the door was a figure far too tall to be Jeremy. She was still hesitating when she heard his voice.

'I know you're standing there. I can summon Jeremy and the police and anyone else I can think of to make a fuss, or you can let me in.'

He sounded calm, almost indifferent, and she wasn't misled for a moment, but she seemed to have run out of options. She reached out to the latch, and stepped back for

173

him to come in.

He looked at her. 'I still prefer my bathrobe to that thing,' he said dispassionately, and watched the colour flare in her cheeks. 'May I come into the flat, or shall we talk here in the shop where everyone can watch?' he asked.

Conscious of the stares she was already receiving through the wide display windows, she turned without a word and walked into the kitchen, all her plans in ruins.

'What do you want?' she asked bluntly when he closed the door behind him.

His dark blue gaze seemed to find her question almost foolish, but she thought he changed his mind about what he was going to say.

'Breakfast,' he said at last. 'I've been travelling since seven-thirty this morning and it's taken me three hours to get here.'

She looked at him helplessly and she saw his eyes narrow as he took in the state of the kitchen. He brushed past her and lifted the empty kettle, then opened a cupboard to disturb a spider.

'When did you last eat?' he demanded.

She shook her head. It was difficult to think with him looming over her, his anger hidden but still there. She hadn't eaten lunch yesterday, or anything since. There had been coffee with him and Val in the morning, but she couldn't remember anything else. He was frowning now, pulling out a chair from the table. He took her shoulders in an almost impersonal clasp and pushed her towards the seat.

'Sit down before you fall down,' he ordered. 'I'm going shopping.' He turned back to the door, adding as he opened it, 'And don't lock me out.'

She hadn't intended to. She had reached the end of her road and stopped running. She supposed she could flee again while he was out, but she didn't think it would be for long and she doubted if she had the energy. If they had to face each other in anger, it might as well be here and now as in a few days' time. Perhaps running had always been a bad idea.

She looked down at herself, conscious of her dishevelled appearance and the advantage if had already given him. With an effort she made her way to the bathroom; she could always use the despised nightshirt as a towel.

She was still in the bath when he came back, and he must have heard her there. He said nothing, but she heard sounds coming from the kitchen and, as she dried herself, the smell of fresh coffee began to tantalise her. She left the scorned nightshirt in a damp heap on the floor and pulled on fresh jeans and a T-shirt. Make-up seemed like too much effort and a defence he would quickly see through, but she plaited her hair severely back, revealing all the fine angles and planes of her face.

His shopping seemed to have been extensive. He had put plain plates and mugs on the table and was pouring coffee from a rather garish jug. The smell of toast was also beginning to tempt her appetite, and there was a boiled egg by her plate. The cutlery was evidently from the camping shop.

He looked up, nothing evident in his face except companionship. 'Not quite Design House, I agree, but it'll do for now. Sit down and eat something.'

At least food was strength, and it gave her something to do with her hands and something to look at besides him.

She didn't realise how hungry she had been until she'd finished her second slice of teast and laced her fingers round the warmth of her mug. That faint dizziness with which she had first seen him probably hadn't just been reaction to his presence, after all. Unfortunately, the return to full awareness had its drawbacks. The most important was her reaction to the figure sitting opposite, watching her as though trying to assess her fitness to cope with whatever he had to say. The silence ceased being a truce and began to fill with tension, until she stood up abruptly and cleared the table, stacking the crockery by the sink.

'We don't even have to wash up,' he said behind her. 'We could simply throw it all out. It won't be much loss.' She didn't respond, still unsure of what his apparent indifference masked. 'I think it's time we talked,' he said at last, his voice quiet but determined.

She turned to face him, glad to be on her feet. At least his height would not dominate her. 'No.' She tried to keep her voice as even as his. 'Don't you see? That's why I left; we'll only end up arguing.'

'Then let's argue. At least that way we're communicating,' he insisted.

'No. And it's not what I'd call communication.'

'There are other ways.' Dark blue eyes challenged her to remember the wordless communication they had found in each other's arms when it had seemed as though minds as well as bodies were in perfect accord.

'No.' If he touched her, if he used that power over her now, she did not think she could bear it, even though her body already knew it would respond helplessly. But he was shaking his head as though in rejection of his own suggestion.

'No,' he agreed. 'It was too special to be used as a weapon, wasn't it?'

He was already using memory and her own weakness to influence her. Two could do that. She met his challenge with one her own. 'Was it? How do I know?' She reminded him deliberately of her own inexperience.

He sighed. 'How indeed? But I think you do,' he added without emphasis. He seemed to be looking for another way of approaching what he wanted to say. 'Let's take this slowly,' he began at last. 'Will you at least promise to tell me the truth if you answer at all?' He must have read her doubt, the knowledge that such a commitment could strip her of all her defences with a few questions. 'All right. But I'll try to be honest with you.'

She wasn't convinced that she wanted honesty. Illusion had its own powerful attractions.

'Don't you even want to know what's happened at the house since you left?' he asked, and she had to fight not to relax at his lighter tone, the implied invitation to share something amusing. 'Not even what I've done to Val?' he suggested.

'You can't blame her,' she began to protest, unwilling to have been the cause of a major row between brother and sister.

He smiled as though welcoming her response. 'She's still alive,' he reassured her. 'By the time I tracked her down, and she wisely didn't return home until late yesterday evening, I already knew you'd taken the London train. What I intended to wring out of her,' he said reminiscently, 'was where you'd gone.'

'But she didn't know,' Olivia protested.

'No. But she still provided me with the confirmation I needed.'

'What do you mean?'

'I thought from the first that you might come here.' He looked around him and said in a more gentle voice, 'It seemed the most obvious bolt-hole—most injured creatures run for home, after all.'

Pity was the last thing she could bear from him. She lifted her chin and gestured to the bareness around her. 'It's not exactly home any more.'

'I know that.' He was watching her intently, and then he

seemed to remember what he'd been saying. 'I still thought you might come here, but then I wondered if you'd realise that I might guess and avoid it. The thought of tracking you through every hotel and boarding-house in or near London daunted even me.' He brushed his hair back from his forehead and she thought suddenly how weary he looked. Then he smiled again, and she thought she must have been mistaken.

'Fortunately, Val was able to tell me, quite defiantly, that not only did she not know where you were, but that she wasn't even expecting to hear from you because you wouldn't have access to a phone. That put the odds on this place in a far better light, and saved me the final humiliation of having to phone your blasted boyfriend to find out if you had turned up. It seemed well worth taking the chance this morning without alerting anyone else. In fact, I nearly came down last night, but thought you'd be even less responsive at three in the morning. If that's possible,' he added as he took in her still face.

Silence had become her only refuge, and even that had its trap. It left far too much scope for that voice to weave its charms yet tighter about her. For want of anything else to do, and because she needed the support, she sat down again.

'You can't imagine what the house was like when it was discovered that you'd gone,' he told her, his tone coaxing her to interest, to memories of the place where she had been both miserable and ecstatic. 'I even began to think,' he went on, 'that perhaps I ought to give in and call it The Folly, after all. Joe was sulking in the garden and looking as though he wanted to put paraquat in my drink; Miss Johnson was about to resign; even Mrs Joe's cooking was below par—at least, nobody ate much of it—and poor Patrick seemed intent on challenging me to a duel.'

feelings definitely *are* involved?' She frowned and he grinned. 'Theresa,' He said cheerfully. She felt her stomach lurch with pain and his expression changed at once. 'I'm sorry, I shouldn't have put it like that. What I'm saying is that I have disliked her thoroughly ever since I employed her two years ago, and it's got worse since she started behaving so stupidly after the divorce. The point is, however, that she *is* still working for me. Now do you believe me?'

It was oddly convincing. If personal feelings hadn't operated in one direction, why should they do so in another? 'But you never seemed to get angry with her,' she argued.

'Until she started harming you, there was nothing to be angry about. Her attempts to lure me into her bed certainly weren't worth it,' he grinned. 'You're the one who manages somehow to make me lose my temper, and that has nothing at all to do with work. It's simply that you won't trust me,' he finished, coming back to his original complaint.

She didn't even trust herself. She had told herself when she first realised who he was that people like Ross Courtenay weren't right for girls like her. She knew why: the gap was too wide. And yet he seemed to be trying to bridge it, and she wanted desperately to believe it was possible.

He may have sensed some weakening in her because he relaxed a little, as though reluctant to overwhelm her with pressure. When he spoke again he had changed the subject slightly and his voice held as much curiosity as anything else.

'Why exactly *did* you run?'

She shrugged. 'There were too many people around. I needed some time alone.'

His smile was sympathetic. 'That's what I thought. Your mistake was in not realising that it was time alone *together* that we needed.' He looked around. 'I can't say I'd have chosen this setting, but it may be for the best, after all.'

His assurance was as difficult to handle as his aggression, but when the knock came at the door and she heard the tinkle of the shop bell, she couldn't help but begin to laugh at the incredulous expression on his face.

'Olivia?' a voice called uncertainly from the shop.

'Jeremy,' she explained, and watched his answering grin fade rapidly. 'He said he'd drop in.'

'Did he?' Ross did not seem to appreciate the neighbourly concern.

'Yes.' She raised her voice. 'In the kitchen, Jeremy,' she called.

He opened the door and was clearly taken aback to find that she was not alone.

'You've met Ross Courtenay, haven't you?' she said, amusement at the antagonism between the two men a relief from the emotional strain of the past hour.

Jeremy nodded and held out his hand. 'How do you do? I didn't know Olivia had company.'

'I arrived this morning.'

Jeremy was obviously ill at ease, uncertain what situation he was interrupting. Olivia almost felt the moment when Ross decided to be charming. He thanked Jeremy, on her behalf, for coming over, and she did not know whether to be indignant or amused as he went on, 'We've both been very grateful for your care for the shop over the past few weeks. It's always good to know someone reliable is looking after something so valuable as a property like this.'

She wanted to hit him for that possessive 'we', and the easy way he had disarmed Jeremy and flattered his vanity. But she also wanted to giggle at the speed with which he had done it.

'It was only the neighbourly thing to do,' Jeremy was agreeing, clearly glad to find Ross so sensible, 'and as you must know, property is so very vulnerable these days. I thought I ought to check up on Olivia, though,' he said, as if, she thought, making an excuse to someone who just might have a right to take offence, 'since her arrival was so unexpected.'

'It was just one of those impulsive things.' If Ross was going to act the responsible guardian, then she might as well be sweetly feminine. She thought she saw his lips twitch, but he reached out to cover her hands with one of his own in a supportive gesture.

'You know how it is,' he said to Jeremy, two men accepting female frailty. 'She knew the place would be sold soon and it has so many memories.'

Of course he understood. She was gratified that the excuse she had planned to use herself was so obviously effective.

Ross did not release her hand and, seeing this, Jeremy cleared his throat. 'I'm glad you're in safe hands, Olivia,' he told her. She didn't know whether to laugh or panic. 'I'll leave you now. Perhaps we'll meet again?' he said to Ross, shaking his hand again.

'Perhaps.' Ross released her to stand up and walk with Jeremy to the door.

She was chuckling when he came back, grinning broadly. 'You're evil, Ross Courtenay,' she accused him.

'Why? It got rid of him, and he even thinks I may not be so bad, after all. It might also,' he said more firmly, 'make up his mind for him at last about who he's going to marry.' He looked at her. 'You wouldn't really have done it, would you?'

'What? Married Jeremy?'

'Yes.'

'I might have done once.' Before I met you, she added to herself. 'I don't know. The idea seemed to have its good points.'

'What, for heaven's sake?'

'Oh, I don't know. Dad would have liked it. I'd have had security, a home, a family of my own.' She had nearly added 'love', but she wasn't certain she had then known what it meant, and it was a dangerous word to use now.

'That's what you want?' She nodded. It was easier than speaking. The humour had faded as quickly as it had come. Now he was looking at her as though he would read her mind. 'So why did you embark on an affair with me?' he asked softly.

It was as though he was pinning her down with the question. Cornered, her response was a challenge of her own, lest she give him the true answer and embarrass them both. 'Isn't it what you always intended? You did warn me, after all, and it wasn't your fault that I didn't believe you.'

His glance did not waver. 'Why did you let yourself be seduced, then?'

'Did I?'

'You're not that naïve.' His voice was still quiet, certain of itself. 'Nor are you so innocent that you didn't realise you should have fled a lot earlier. It would have made more sense.'

She looked down at her hands, fighting the scarlet tide she could feel in her cheeks. He was right. She had known the risk she was running, if not its full extent, and had deliberately courted the fire that had scorched her. Humiliation at least gave her a last flare of saving anger. She glared back up at him.

'What are you trying to make me say? That I can't control my reactions to you? You know that's true. How do you think that makes me feel?'

'That's what I want to know. I know how it makes me feel.'

'Like some sort of self-satisfied sultan, I should think,' she snapped at him, and he gave a sudden, half-smothered laugh.

'I meant my own uncontrollable reaction to you,' he explained, still laughing. He met her look of total disbelief and smiled so that her bones seemed to melt. 'Poor innocent. You didn't stand a chance, did you? Look,' he said, serious again, 'I promise I'll leave you alone—preferably at Val's or a hotel,' he added, looking around, 'but can't we just have one more try to get this ridiculous tangle sorted out?'

It was too simple. She watched him warily. If she knew one thing about Ross Courtenay designs, it was that their simplicity was always deceptive.

'What do you mean?'

'Can we go back to the job you won't take?'

'You know about that,' she reminded him.

'I know it originally had nothing to do with Theresa's comments—you'd already turned it down by then.'

'And I told you why.'

'And even when I'd recovered my temper I didn't believe you. I still don't. Are you afraid of it? Or is it what Val suggested, that it's a loss of independence?'

He had been right about one thing: this time honesty was necessary. She could no longer lie to him. 'No, it was nothing like that. Val's idea never crossed my mind.'

'Then what was it?'

He would have to know at least half the truth. 'Because you seemed to be taking over my life,' she admitted.

'What's wrong with that? You're taking over mine.' His smile was very gentle. 'So you'll run away instead? Leave me in the lurch, with our affair and your job unfinished, and even letting someone else take the credit for your discovery?'

She ignored the provocation, sidetracked for the moment by this reminder of the book she had almost forgotten.

'Did he ring?' she demanded. 'What did he say?'

He sighed, but sounded amused by her eagerness. 'Yes, he

rang. Yes, you are almost certainly right. And now can we forget it?'

'But it's——'

'I know exactly what it is. I've lived without that book before and I could quite easily do so again. I do not, however, feel the same way about you,' he added with great patience.

'What?' It was hardly elegant, but she thought she must have misunderstood.

'If ever again,' he said carefully, 'I try to restrain myself because of your youth and inexperience, not to mention my own doubts about your feelings, remind me to ask Val, or even Patrick, to step in and run my life. He can't decide whether he wants to give you away or be best man, by the way.'

She stared at him, unable to equate what he was saying with the way he was saying it.

He reached out and traced the line of her jaw. 'Is the silence a sign of brain-softening? Brought on, I rather desperately hope, by a suspected case of unrequited love? I do love you, you know. I want to marry you. Will you please put me out of my misery and tell me you feel something similar?'

'You love me?' It couldn't be true, but he was looking at her in a way she had never seen before, and his face was wholly vulnerable.

'Yes.' Its simplicity convinced her utterly.

She looked down at her hands, picking up a teaspoon and fiddling with it until his hand over hers stilled them.

'Olivia?'

It was a demand for an answer, and she suddenly realised he was uncertain. All she could give him was the truth he had asked for so much earlier.

'The reason I wouldn't take the job, the real reason,' she said carefully, not looking at him, 'was that I didn't think I could survive being with you unless I could get away quickly and spare us both the pain and embarrassment of your knowing that I love you more than life itself.'

She was in his arms, held tightly against him with a desperation that matched her own. Too intent on holding each other even to kiss at first, she felt his hand move in her hair. His voice was shaken when at last he spoke, but the laughter was back.

'I've always suspected self-sacrifice was misguided. We've both been idiots. If I forgive you your simple-mindedness, will you forgive me mine?'

'You warned me about the insanity in your family,' she reminded him, 'and I think it was too late even then.'

'Good.' His hand in her hair persuaded her to lift her head, and she met his kiss without reserve.

Their fear of rejection was too recent, their love too newly declared, for one kiss to be enough. She was as eager as he when he broke off to murmur, 'Did you have a bed last night?'

'Of sorts.'

She took him to her bedroom and he surveyed the untidy mattress with amusement. 'Your taste in furnishing seems to have deteriorated,' he commented. 'But I'm sure we'll manage.'

He took her back in his arms and she both yielded to his demands and made such ardent claims of her own that neither of them noticed the discomforts of the bedding until they woke much later, still in close embrace.

She moved against him with contentment and he chuckled. 'Stiff?' he asked. She stretched experimentally.

'Not at all. It must have been the bed's fault last time,' she decided.

'Possibly. But, much as I love you——' The words still had

the power to shake her, and she turned her mouth against his naked shoulder and felt his response to her kiss. 'Much as I love you,' he repeated, the strain of control showing slightly as she continued to explore his body, 'I have no intention of importing this mattress into our home. Stop that,' he lifted her head and kissed her quickly, adding, 'for the moment, anyway. Tell me why you wouldn't let yourself believe I could love you?' His regret for her recent suffering was clear.

'Tell me why you said you intended to seduce me,' she said, and saw that he understood that she had believed this had been a statement of the limit of his intentions.

'Family lunacy, I suspect. Oh, in a way it was true to start with, although I doubt if what I felt was ever that simple. It certainly put up all your defences, and I suppose that's partly what I intended. You were so vulnerable, and I knew how badly I wanted you, and I half thought someone ought to warn you against me. You undermined all my self-control, you see. Perhaps there was an element of self-preservation in it, too,' he admitted. 'I was almost afraid of what was happening to me, and not at all sure that I wanted to have to cope with something that looked as though it might have been very serious indeed.'

'Theresa would have been much simpler,' agreed Olivia happily, full of contentment and aware of passion just below the surface of their words.

'Theresa,' he said carefully, 'made her expectations so blindingly obvious that I was bored almost before she began. You,' he trailed a finger between her breasts and watched her changed breathing, 'could never bore me. You might drive me finally into insanity, but I'll take the risk.'

'Good.'

'You know,' he said, 'it should all have been so easy. From the moment I saw you I just wanted to pick you up off that

pavement and take you home with me. But then I discovered
you were already engaged, and it seemed that it must be all
one-sided, after all.' She remembered Val's comments; so she
hadn't been wrong. 'And then,' he went on, 'your father died
and I still wasn't sure if you were heartbroken about Jeremy
or not.'

'And I thought you'd taken me on as some sort of charity
case whom you happened to fancy,' she admitted.

'I certainly fancied you.' His grin was full of promise. 'But
there was no question of charity. In fact I'm beginning to
wonder how the house and firm ran before you arrived. Miss
Johnson told me why you were acting as secretary that day,
you know. She thinks a lot of you. I think Joe will go into
mourning and cut down the roses if you don't come back.
And Patrick probably *will* branch out on his own, be
fabulously successful, and I'll go bankrupt. So can you see
that I really do need you?' he ended, only half teasing.

'I'm beginning to.'

'Good. Then it's time to get up.' He stood up and she
enjoyed the sight of his long, naked body, not troubling to
hide her appreciation. 'Don't look at me like that or we'll
never get where we're going, and I don't want to spend the
night on dust sheets.' He reached down, pulling her up to him
with that easy strength which had always impressed her.

'Where are we going?' She didn't really care.

'To the nearest hotel for tonight. Not the Crown,' he
amended. 'And then to the London flat for that week alone we
keep planning.'

'I haven't got any clothes,' she objected without conviction.

'You won't need any. Now, will you come with me?'

'Anywhere.' And it was a commitment for both of them,
for life.